DEFIANT SPACE

INFINITE VOID BOOK ONE

RICHARD RIMINGTON

Join our newsletter for exclusive access to 'The Survivors' - a prologue short story to the Infinite Void series.

Plus early reading access, discounts on new releases, and more exclusive bonus content:

Join here:
https://cutt.ly/rimington

The characters and events portrayed in this book are fictitious. Any similarity to real persons, living or dead, is coincidental and not intended by the author.

No part of this book may be reproduced, or stored in a retrieval system, or transmitted in any form or by any means, electronic, mechanical, photocopying, recording, or otherwise, without express written permission of the publisher.

Copyright © 2021 Richard Rimington

All rights reserved.

ISBN: 9798758231180

Dedicated to Indrani,

A person of cosmic importance.

CONTENTS

Chapter 1	Pg 7
Chapter 2	Pg 22
Chapter 3	Pg 41
Chapter 4	Pg 50
Chapter 5	Pg 65
Chapter 6	Pg 81
Chapter 7	Pg 97
Chapter 8	Pg 113
Chapter 9	Pg 136
Chapter 10	Pg 152
Chapter 11	Pg 166
Chapter 12	Pg 180
Chapter 13	Pg 199
Chapter 14	Pg 214
Epilogue	Pg 236
Infinite Void Series	Pg 248
Acknowledgements	Pg 255

Chapter 1

In space, a trio of warships came for Vale Reach like silent predators prowling in the night. The ships were privateer vessels, dispatched to issue the demands of some higher authority. They advanced toward their prey without hesitation, gliding through the vacuum like an arrow racing to strike its target. Each ship bristled with an assortment of weapons, primed and ready. Their metal hulls were as dark as coal yet gleamed along one flank, reflecting the white light of the system's primary sun. The star system they entered was devoid of any surveillance stations or defense satellites that could have warned the local population of the intruders who roamed unopposed.

Vale Reach was the only inhabited planet in this place. Its lands were still green, its skies clear and calm. The citizens on its surface had no understanding of the terrible danger now approaching. The warships took up positions in high orbit, triangulated around Vale Reach. As the entire planet fell under the shadow of their judgment, they began to transmit a message.

Across every communications channel on the world below, the signal became distorted and then blank. In its place, a new voice emerged through the static, speaking in a language none of the people could understand. The tone of the words was harsh and threatening, echoing through every office and home across the planet.

The warships fell silent. Days went by. The warships remained, waiting in the vast, empty blackness, ready to impose a sentence of death at any sign of defiance from below.

*

Councilor Theeran stood on a balcony, high on the central tower of the Unification Palace in Vale Reach's capital city, Arkstone. He was fifty years old, with hair rapidly turning from gray to white. The midmorning sounds of the city reached Theeran as a soft murmur from his position up on the balcony. In general, life in this city had progressed at a sedate pace for years. No longer would that be the case. That much was certain.

The structure of the Unification Palace was a glorious monument of red marble and orthogonal edges, the finest building of its kind on all Vale Reach, filled with soaring archways and complex mosaic patterns best viewed from his current position. Theeran was prepared to use everything at his disposal to make the right impression on his off-world guest. He wore the full regalia of his office, civilian honors in the form of gold chains. Theeran watched as a small shuttlecraft descended through the skies and landed on the small platform for aircraft on the palace roof. His visitor was not from the dreaded warships that lurked above. They were a third party, an adjudicator. Theeran recognized nothing about the shuttle. It was entirely foreign to his world. The skies above Arkstone were normally empty except for birds. Theeran felt a sense of careful anticipation. No one from outside Vale Reach had set foot on this world in many years.

Theeran heard the echo of feet walking on the hard marble floor as his guest approached. The double doors leading to the balcony creaked open, and a small middle-aged man in a loose-fitting blue suit walked out to join him. The visitor's shoulders were slightly hunched, and he shuffled as he moved.

"My goodness! That's a truly unique shuttle pad you've got up there. I've never encountered one so very minimalist," the man said. He carried a bundle of documents under each arm. With a sigh, the newcomer dropped his files onto a table by the balcony and turned to take a look out across the city. "Very nice. A pleasure to be here." He leaned on the balcony's railing and took in his surroundings. After a few seconds, he seemed satisfied. "My name is Advocate Fargas, and I will be your legal counsel for the next stage of your proposed appeals." He hesitated slightly. "To be frank, the odds are definitely against you. I apologize if I start to have an allergic reaction, by the way. I honestly hate making an abrupt entry into new planets, but they told me your case was an emergency, and who can say no to that?"

"To call it an emergency is accurate," Theeran said grimly. "My name is Councilor Theeran. I am a special coordinator for the Vale Reach intelligence services, based out of the Unification Palace here. We're lucky the privateer ships in orbit allowed you past."

"They have to let me past. I'm a registered legal counsel," said Advocate Fargas.

"Would you care for some refreshments?" asked Councilor Theeran. At that moment, a butler from the Unification Palace emerged through the doorway to the balcony, carrying a tray full of drinks.

Fargas looked appreciative and took one of the tall, elegant glasses.

As Fargas sipped the drink, Theeran continued, "Before we go any further, I must ask a question of you. Forgive my bluntness, but it can't be avoided. Given that we have no means of offering you any compensation, what exactly is your motivation for assisting us?"

The palace butler retreated back indoors.

"Well," Advocate Fargas said as he spread out his folders on the small table and extracted some papers, "it's an unfortunate story. You could say I'm currently on probation for some very minor offences. Intoxication. Disorderly conduct. Harmless stuff, but apparently, it all adds up."

The man seemed calm and unconcerned, which was jarring with the knot of tension Theeran felt in his own stomach. He waited for the man to conclude his explanation.

Fargas continued to talk as he organized his notes. "Taking on a case as unwanted as yours is an officially recognized act of charity amongst the interstellar legal community. When I heard about your situation, I knew I had to come. We both benefit from this, you and I. You gain my services as a legal counsel, which are very badly needed, in all likelihood, and I pay restitution for my so-called misdeeds and return to a good standing among my peers."

Theeran continued to study the man, looking at his skin and his clothes. He looked at the weave of the fibers in the fabric of the man's blue suit, noticing countless small surface differences between the lawyer and himself, as though they were made of entirely different forms of matter. Being in the presence of an offworlder again, after so many years, was fascinating. Theeran had met offworlders before, decades ago, as part of his work in Vale Reach intelligence. He knew from experience how very similar to themselves the offworlders really were. He suspected human nature changed very little from planet to planet.

"Shall we begin a review of the key points?" asked Fargas. "Your case has been thrown out by a long list of appeals courts so far. Congratulations on continuing regardless. I do admire your persistence. You're really fighting your case to the bitter end. Have you received a translated copy of Legion's message yet?"

"On behalf of Hardline Interstellar, a registered subsidiary of the Universal Legion, we issue notice this planet has been declared vital territory in the war of Humanity against the Makron Empire," Councilor Theeran repeated from memory. "The Universal Legion asserts the right to begin construction of any required assets on and around the planets of this system. Any resistance will be regarded as an act of high treason. Acknowledge your submission or suffer the consequences."

Fargas looked out and admired the view of Arkstone again. It was a city built low and flat, so the view from Unification Palace stretched across many miles of rooftops. "Lovely place here," Fargas said again. "So. The Universal Legion is annexing your entire planet owing to the pending threat of large-scale war with the Makron Empire in this region. You're appealing to halt their operation, probably by obtaining an injunction that will prevent the loss of your sovereignty. But no one issues decrees like that against the Universal Legion. By any conventional analysis, the courts have not listened favorably to any of your arguments thus far. The consensus is that you have no right to reject their presence. Your case has already passed through all available stages of arbitration, and they've all ruled against you, before I was even aware of the situation. But why do I feel you're about to tell me there's another option remaining?"

"That is correct," Theeran said.

The sky above them grew slightly brighter as morning became midday. The breeze around the balcony was still cool.

"I can understand why you're determined not to quit," said Fargus. "There are many good reasons to be afraid of the Universal Legion." He placed several small devices on the table that projected holographic displays up into the air. He followed with a series of specific hand gestures, and the holographic displays turned into detailed video recordings. "The Legion has done this many times before. Nobody knows how old they are, but I can tell you, from their size alone, that events like this happen regularly."

The holograms displayed dozens of planets floating above the balcony's railing.

"The Legion reaches from one edge of the galactic disk to the other, in some form. They claim your whole planet is required for the war against the Makron. There are clear precedents for what that looks like," said Fargas.

The holograms shifted to show rocky terrain with what appeared to be a black flat-topped volcano at its center, blasting a torrent of gray ash into the air. On closer view, Theeran saw the volcano was actually a man-made structure, with orange lights blinking across its surface.

"Mineral harvesting for the rapid extraction of geological assets," Fargas said.

He snapped his fingers. The holograms changed to hills and green jungle, viewed from high above. The trees seemed to twist and writhe as explosions tore through the foliage. Blue plasma fire erupted.

"Live fire maneuvers, often against captured enemy combatants," Fargas continued. "And finally, perhaps the most severe outcome of all, total fortification and emplacement as a battleground."

At first, the holograms appeared to show a maze, a geometric pattern of white fractal lines against black. It was concrete and shadow, Theeran realized, row after row of bunkers and trenches. The camera panned out to reveal the earth around as a shocking fluorescent yellow, stained by caustic chemical weapons. Mushroom clouds towered high on the horizon.

"The Universal Legion is, when all is said and done, one of the most formidable fighting machines in the galaxy," said Fargas. "If the Makron Empire ever does come here, and I doubt they will, the Legion will split this planet to its core before they admit defeat."

Councilor Theeran shook his head in dismay. "If our planet becomes another vassal in their possession, we potentially face absolute destruction." He was emphatic as he voiced his deepest fear.

"Now, I hate to bring this up," said Fargas, "but as your case is officially a charitable cause, I have to assume you have no interstellar currency or assets of notable value? Nothing any other empires or states might recognize as a demanded resource?"

Councilor Theeran sighed. "You've answered your own question there. We receive no interstellar trade. We have only our own very modest natural resources to work with."

Fargas sighed. "You're definitely one of the more low-tech clients I've worked with. Your orbital space is as quiet as a graveyard, except for the intruders. I saw nothing moving up there. There are two transit points at the edge of your star system, as usual. I saw a handful of freighters passing through on their way somewhere, but otherwise, you're essentially considered a patch of empty space." An awkward silence occurred. "Sorry," Fargus said, "I know people don't like hearing things like that. But being poor will drastically harm your odds of being heard. Litigation against the military is tough at the best of times. If you're a nobody, then it's going to be essentially impossible."

"We're going to the Ruarken High Senate," said Councilor Theeran.

Fargas stood up from leaning on the railing. "That's a bold move," he said, seeming genuinely surprised. "The Ruarken High Senate could be one of the few people in the galaxy who might take serious action on your case. They openly hate the Universal Legion. They have for centuries now, due to the usual indiscretions and atrocities on the Legion's part. But the Ruarken High Senate is sixty thousand light-years away. You do know they only accept petitions that are submitted in person, in front of legal witnesses?" said Fargas. "And you don't have any starships that could take you there. You specifically aren't allowed them."

"Due to the Binding Treaty," said Theeran. He paused for a moment, his frustration almost becoming visible. "A gift left to us by our last occupiers, the Sirkallions. Are you familiar with it?"

"I've read it. Under the terms your world signed eighty years ago, in exchange for the Sirkallions granting your independence, you were banned from developing fusion reactors, starships... pretty much anything beyond basic electrical power. There's also a blacklist to stop any form of travel visa being issued to your citizens, preventing you from leaving your world. It's a grim document. I feel a little hopeless just looking at it. Why did you ever agree to this?""

"At the time, it was a guarantee of peace." Theeran tapped his hands on the marble railing. "Eighty years ago, our planet was a vassal of the Sirkallion Empire. The demands for the independence of the people of Vale Reach were reaching a boiling point. The level of anger on the street couldn't be contained anymore. People were rioting. Society was close to collapse. When the Sirkallions offered the Binding Treaty in exchange for their withdrawal, it seemed like a miracle. We could finally have independence. The level of isolation dictated by the treaty was even seen as desirable by some of us. Of course, being unable to develop our technology was a handicap, but the government of the era judged accepting the treaty to be the only possible way to avoid terrible bloodshed. If we hadn't signed it, the people here would have begun a war against the Sirkallion garrisons, and the gods alone know where that would have taken us."

"Well, what happens if you break the treaty now?" asked Fargas. "What if we were to hypothetically make a breakout attempt to try to bring Vale Reach up to a higher level of tech?"

Theeran grimaced in distaste. "The Sirkallion Empire sends inspection teams to our world—every year according to their calendar, which is nearly every two of our years. If they don't like what they see… air strikes, usually. 'Destruction of prohibited sites' is their term. Potentially, they can expand on that to a full military occupation of our surface, according to how they interpret the treaty. Since this dispute with Universal Legion started, the Sirkallions have indicated a clear willingness to fully comply with any of the Legion's demands. If they seize control again, then it's all finished. Reports indicate that the Sirkallion Empire has just purchased a complete new inventory of military hardware from Universal Legion, which I'm sure is no coincidence."

"Indeed. From what I can tell, not a single one of your neighbors is willing to back you up on this issue," said Fargas. "They're all ready to comply with the Legion. I can tell you that some of their worlds have already been seized too. They don't want to antagonize the Legion further." He gave a small shrug. "You're surrounded by hostile interests on all sides," he said. "Anyone could potentially sell you out to the Legion if they detect a breach in the treaty. It would seem you are trapped here."

"Getting to the Ruarken High Senate will be the most vital part of our task," said Theeran. He scrutinized Fargas for any significant reaction to this statement.

Nothing.

"How much does the general population of your world know about all this?" Fargas asked.

"They have no way of understanding the message that everyone received," said Theeran. "Even here at the Ruling Council, we had to request a translation from outside the Vale Reach star system. Obviously, people are keenly aware that something's wrong. The Universal Legion managed to strike fear even through the language barrier. It's a mercy that most people remain unaware of the true state of things. People only know that there was an invasive transmission and that it almost certainly came to us from space. That's more than enough. They're all afraid, of course. Plenty of theories have appeared so far, a few of which are partially correct. A few amateur astronomers have even been able to physically sight the Legion vessels in orbit above, but since the warships have insulated their radio signals, they remain unidentifiable. The contents of the message are unknown except to us here at the palace. I have a suspicion the Legion simply couldn't be bothered trying to figure out what language we actually speak."

"Actually this isn't even the proper Legion you're dealing with," said Fargas. "They've sent a minion to handle you, a subcontractor named Hardline Interstellar. But that doesn't matter for now. Any activity from the warships since the message?"

"From what we can tell, they are simply waiting, either for a response from us, or a response from their masters. Perhaps the Legion pays them by the hour if they are a sub-contractor, as you say," said Theeran with a degree of bitterness. He considered how the demise of their world was just regular business for someone else.

"Perhaps they do." Advocate Fargas laughed for a second as he considered it. "So what's the plan if you do reach the Ruarken High Senate? Bring me in on your argument." He raised his eyebrows. "What do you have that will actually convince the Ruarken Senate to back your petition and rule against the Legion? Why should they get involved?"

"There's no point getting on our knees and crying for mercy," said Theeran. "That's surely all been heard before. If we come to the Senate with nothing more than ideas about liberty and justice, our hearing won't last more than a minute." He paused for a moment. "Yet despite the immense odds against us, we cannot submit to the inevitable. If Vale Reach were to accept a slow colonization as a compromise, it'd begin an era that'd never end. The changes would be irreversible. So we have no choice but to resist the Legion at all costs. But if we demand our own autonomy and die with dignity and honor, what is the prize for us then?" Theeran paused again then spoke carefully. "If we reach the Ruarken High Senate and we receive nothing, and we're all personally destroyed, then at least our appeal will have been seen by the many spectators of the Ruarken Senate. Our testimony being on the record will strengthen the petitions of those who come after us. Our only path is to hope that our case is surely one among many, and that together with all the others that have come before and will come after, we'll collectively have the power to overturn the way things are done. If only we can show people the truth of what is happening, then all this endless tyranny and fear won't be needed. To believe otherwise is to accept inevitable defeat. Our task may be immeasurable in its scale, but for our world to live, there is no alternative."

Advocate Fargas rubbed his head and nodded, frowning slightly as he absorbed the message. "Not too bad. Not too bad. You do a solid job covering up the fact that you've got absolutely nothing. We'll workshop it together. Don't worry. I can tell it's not your first time giving that performance."

Theeran hesitated in surprise. Fargas was right. "I admit it's taken a little work already to convince the rest of the Vale Reach leadership to see things my way," Theeran said. "But I have assembled a project that will change the situation." He decided it was time to show his hand to the offworlder, despite the risk. "There is already a plan in motion for sending envoys from Vale Reach to the Ruarken High Senate, including me and, of course, you too, Advocate Fargas."

"I'm impressed," said Fargas. "But how would I fit into this plan?" He was a small man, and slightly wrinkled with age, but Theeran knew better than to underestimate what he might be capable of.

"Mr. Fargas, how many planets have you visited in your lifetime?" Theeran asked.

Fargas smiled, enjoying the question. His modesty was a façade. "Around three hundred, maybe three hundred and twenty." He gave a little shrug.

Theeran gave no sign of the wonder he felt. "And, Mr. Fargas," he continued, "how many standard years old are you?"

Fargas waved a hand as though embarrassed, but his face had a wide grin as he spoke. "I like to think I don't look it, but my age is also fairly close to three hundred at this point. I visit a decent clinic. They have reasonable rates for my treatments, and they accept my professional insurance package. I honestly can't take much credit for my fine health."

"Then I'm sure you can see, Mr. Fargas, why your expertise will be needed on our mission."

"There's one final problem, and this might be the most unpredictable of all," said Fargas, his eyes seeming more animated.

He's starting to believe that the mission is possible, Theeran thought.

"Vale Reach is situated in an extremely bad neighborhood," Fargas said. "There are active criminal organizations claiming territory for hundreds of lights around. They generally harass civilian shipping however they choose. I won't make any presumptions as to how you may be leaving this planet, but regardless, the constant presence of outlaw starships is something you're going to have to deal with. Space here is dangerously unregulated."

Theeran looked out into the streets of Arkstone. Vehicle traffic flowed smoothly through the streets. Sunlight glinted from the flat paving tiles. He would be leaving it all behind soon.

"Void pirates," he said slowly.

"Pirates, reavers, and corsairs, yes. In plentiful amounts," said Fargas.

"They are certainly a severe threat," said Theeran. "We've planned for their potential impact as best we can."

Dwelling on the chances of violent destruction was something he tried to avoid. Death awaited them in so many ways.

"Perhaps worse for you are the mercenary fleets that are guarding the planets against the pirates," said Fargas. "They've spread throughout space here to keep the pirates at bay, and nearly all of these military units are registered franchisees of the Universal Legion, much like Hardline Interstellar above us now. If any of them intercept you, then the Universal Legion will become aware of your plan and will very likely accelerate their timetable for the reconstruction of this planet."

"Then I'm sure you agree," Theeran said, "that subterfuge is our only option. We need to proceed undetected throughout our journey."

Fargas nodded in agreement. "Subterfuge is indeed your only option, but that can't last forever."

"It doesn't need to. Only until we reach the Great Highway," Theeran said.

The Highway was the frontier of their knowledge. Under Theeran's orders, researchers had found long-abandoned star charts in the museums of Arkstone, which had been used to verify reports of what was ahead. They'd determined that the Great Highway at Thelmia would transport them far across the galaxy, leaving behind all the dangers they faced in their home sector.

"The Highway will take us beyond the reach of our enemies here. If we reach the Highway, we can get far from the pirate clans and also exit the jurisdiction of the mercenary groups in this region. I'm not claiming things will be smooth on the other side, but at least if we get caught after the Highway, we'll be far harder to identify. No one has heard of Vale Reach on the other side."

Fargas smiled and stroked his chin. "Subterfuge until the Grand Highway? It could work."

"It has to work."

Fargas reached out and shook hands with Theeran. "Fortune favors the bold."

"Tell me what a possible resolution to our case might look like, Mr. Fargas," Theeran said. "Something that allows us to retain control over our own lives."

"In response to your petition, the Ruarken Senate could issue a protection decree that endorses your sovereignty and orders an end to any foreign occupations." Fargas leaned back slightly as he spoke. "You're asking them to no longer tolerate the Universal Legion's so-called emergency measures. That would overturn centuries of policy and earn the Ruarken the extreme displeasure of the Universal Legion. Your nation has no experience arguing cases before any of the Ruarken courts, let alone the High Session of the Ruarken Imperial Senate." He paused and spread his arms wide as though absorbing the sunlight of Vale Reach. "You'll certainly be in need of a lawyer with a talent for delivering the unconventional. I'm the only person on this planet who even speaks a language they understand." Fargas let his arms fall to his sides and patted his files and folders in readiness. "Win or lose, we're going to make some waves."

Chapter 2

Caladon and Eevey were lying together on their bed. The mattress was soft beneath them and warm in the white morning light. Their duvet was on the floor.

"I think today is going to be a perfect day," Eevey said.

They were both in their early twenties and naked. Eevey's hair was black, the same as Cal's. His eyes were closed, and he was comfortably somewhere between sleeping and waking. His mind felt entirely blank. It was midday, Cal guessed, and he had no plans for the afternoon. The street below was quiet, and their apartment felt absolutely still.

Cal opened his eyes. Eevey was lying on her front. He looked at her smooth, long legs. Her skin seemed to glow from the bright daylight flooding into their apartment through the small room's wide-open windows. Perhaps he did have one plan for the day, he decided. Eevey looked back at him. She might find some reason to leave bed and be productive soon. Cal had a better idea. He knew exactly how to delay her.

A rattle sounded at their door.

"What's that?" Eevey asked, turning away.

Cal's brain was sluggish, and his thoughts came gradually. He'd received mail. He rolled over and sat up. "A package arrived."

"Did you order anything?" asked Eevey.

"With my generous academic's salary?"

He stared at the object now on his floor. It was a cylinder, metallic at both ends, weighty looking. Cal hesitated as a sense of wariness suddenly developed. The package was an intruder into his life. There was minimal chance it contained anything good. Cal stared at it and reached out to stroke Eevey's back to soothe his nerves. He considered his options as he searched for a way to avoid opening the package. Eventually, his curiosity got the better of him.

Cal slowly got out of bed and walked across the room. He picked up the cylinder and assessed it. It was hollow, from the weight of it, and made of smoothly machined metal, with electronics as part of it—some kind of container. It was beautiful too. Some prestigious entity had issued it. The tube had a fingerprint scanner at one end. He wondered if it had been built for only him to open. Cal put his thumb on the device, which unlocked at his touch.

"Who sent that?" Eevey asked from across the small room.

Cal opened the cylinder and took out a paper document. "I can't imagine," he said. He sat on the corner of the bed, hesitating to unfold the paper.

Eevey sat up next to him. "Open it. Let's see."

He took a quick breath to settle his nerves before reading the letter.

Eevey leaned in and read it with him. They got to the end and sat in silence. Each of them waited for the other to say something.

"I think they're right," Cal said eventually. His hand was shaking as he held the letter. It had told him of the impending threat of invasion to their world. He put it down. "We already knew that message came from space. And we knew whoever sent it to us did so very intentionally. And we knew they likely weren't sending us a friendly greeting. Everything this letter tells us about the threat our world faces... I think it's all true."

"What are you going to do?" Eevey asked.

The letter was calling on him to help. The government of Vale Reach had selected him for his expertise. In his spare time, Cal had already published several scientific papers describing his theories that attempted to understand the transit points using what little data Vale Reach had. Some set of principles governed their operation, but as with so many things, even Vale Reach's best minds could offer no answers. Cal felt certain he was on the brink of developing a method to determine where any transit point would lead. Of course, he'd never had a way to test it. It was all entirely theoretical.

"They need me to join their project. They want me on a team that's attempting to navigate the interstellar transit network," Cal said.

"Which means you'd be going to space," Eevey said.

Cal lay on his back and stared at the ceiling as his heartrate accelerated. His palms were slightly sweaty. "That could go very badly indeed."

She lay down next to him as they looked at each other. "You don't have to go," she told him.

"I know," he said. "I know." But knowing it was his choice didn't solve anything.

She was watching him.

"But they have a point," Cal said. "If everyone on Vale Reach buries their head in the sand, we might wake up one day to find this place being demolished. They say they need me for this project." He could tell Eevey agreed with what he was saying though she wouldn't say it. "I think... I think everyone in the world might need me to be part of this."

Cal gazed at every detail of her face. He wanted to remember this morning with her forever.

If Vale Reach successfully jumped a starship beyond the home system, the chances of them coming back alive were almost none. Cal knew that. He became resigned to it as he considered the facts. Anyone who studied the evidence could see the galaxy was a hostile and savage place. Yet if his life was to be traded for the fate of their whole world, he didn't see that he really had a choice. He had to go. He had to protect Eevey. He couldn't stay behind and wait for the planet to be destroyed. Everything as he knew it was over.

He put his hands around Eevey and held tight. They stayed in bed for the rest of the day.

*

Far above the surface of Vale Reach, Major Nurten Rosco floated as smoothly as he could through the corridors of the moon base. Gravity was minimal. His was in his late thirties, with a close-shaved military haircut that was just developing its first gray hairs. His complexion was rough from months spent out on army maneuvers in the mountains of Vale Reach. Rosco was impatient to discover why he'd been summoned so far, to the moon, of all places. Supposedly, nothing was at the site beyond a simple industrial refinery. Like all of Vale Reach, he'd heard the hostile transmission they'd received from space. His gut told him the message and his journey were related, yet he was uncomfortable at being ignorant of his mission. A series of small settlements existed on the lunar surface, built by the Vale Reach government for mining operations, plus a handful of satellites for their global communications network, but the facilities were unremarkable. Rosco knew they didn't bring military personnel into orbit for any sort of regular maintenance work. During the few brief hours he'd been at the moon base so far, he'd seen several other high-ranking officers floating in the narrow, unfamiliar corridors. The lack of gravity made him feel unbearably awkward. Ten years in the Vale Reach army had given Rosco strong muscles, but without a hard ground beneath his feet, he moved in a bumbling and uncoordinated fashion, constantly clinging to the walls. He pushed open a set of double doors and froze in shock.

He was floating at one end of a vast hangar bay, a structure that seemed many times larger than the moon base he'd seen. It had been excavated down into the lunar surface, he realized. In front of him, filling the entire space, was a starship nearly a kilometer long in his estimation. Rosco floated near the tip of the ship so that he was looking down its whole length. It was cylindrical, with narrow ends like a cigar and with many vents and hatches across its surface. Rosco was awestruck by the incredible magnitude of the vessel. He counted launch bays, probes, waste ports, even at least one small weapon turret. The engines would be out of sight at the far side. The ship made him feel small like an ant. His eyes adjusted to fully comprehend its length, and he felt a strange sense of vertigo even in the low gravity. It was a skyscraper lying on its side.

The nature of his task changed radically in his mind. Vale Reach had built the ship, he realized. In secret. A word was painted in large letters on the side: *Fidelity*. His people had used every scrap of knowledge they had to construct this vessel. He could see it in the rivets and the bolts holding the ship together. It was no import, nor was it stolen. The ship's existence opened up endless dangers and endless possibilities for their world.

A few years back, Rosco had studied the information Vale Reach intelligence had on the occasional foreign ships that passed through their star system's edge. He now wished he'd paid far more attention. It'd seemed frivolous knowledge, never something he would need. It probably would have done little to prepare him for this encounter. Three hundred people would be needed to crew it, at least, based on what he remembered. The Binding Treaty was in tatters. Maintaining secrecy was paramount. Vale Reach's one and only starship had already changed the situation forever. There would be no going back.

His heart rate accelerated. If the Treaty was broken, then the political situation had deteriorated far beyond what the Ruling Council government allowed people to know. Vale Reach was risking extreme penalties if the ship's construction ever became known. Rosco suddenly realized that the word *Fidelity* on the ship's hull was expanding. That was impossible. It was rendered in paint. Rosco realized he was drifting toward the ship.

"Shit," he muttered to himself, looking around.

He instinctively kicked around for a moment with no change in direction. He'd already floated too far away from the hangar wall to grab anything and stop himself. No railings were within reach, leaving him incapable of altering his path. Rosco rotated a few times and noticed other officers in the hangar bay were already watching him disapprovingly. He felt ridiculous and decided it was better to drift with dignity. Rosco adopted a purposeful pose and waited as he very gradually approached the side of the ship. After a few long minutes, he eventually contacted the metal hull. Rosco gripped it, his hands sliding slightly on the flat surface, but he stopped himself at last. A hatch opened next to him, and a man with reflective silver streaks in his long hair leaned out and studied him.

"You look slightly lost," the man said.

"Who are you?" asked Rosco.

The person he met didn't look like a member of the military.

"I'm the pilot," he said. "Do yourself a favor, and don't tell anyone you met me." His nonchalant tone suggested he didn't much care.

Rosco studied him curiously. "Are you from Vale Reach?" he asked.

The man shook his head. "I think of myself as more of a freelancer. My name's Marraz. We're not supposed to speak to each other."

Rosco considered him for a moment while still awkwardly clinging to the side of the ship. "Then why are you telling me this?" he asked.

The man with reflective hair seemed pleased with the question. "I'm just a compulsive rule breaker."

*

Leda Palchek closed the front door to her apartment for the last time. She'd been renting the place for a few years, but she would have no need of it anymore. In the gray early-morning light, the hallway of her apartment building was filled with deep shadows. She didn't feel any regret as she sealed away her old life. Leda turned the key in the lock, and a sense of relief came over her. She'd already shipped her belongings to a new destination. Leda put her key into the security guard's mailbox and stepped outside into the sunlight. She began the familiar walk across the city to her office. Leda was dressed for a day at her workplace. Her long hair was as untidy as always. The sun's rays were creeping up above the concrete towers of Arkstone and filling the streets, and Leda paced quickly along the empty sidewalks. Today was her final day in the city, but her feet kept their usual fast rhythm out of habit. Soon, she approached the broad glass tower where she had worked for several years. Leda was an engineer at one of the largest research groups on Vale Reach, as part of several teams assigned to unlocking the secrets of the outside universe without breaking the Binding Treaty. The goal had been to develop improved technologies using the simple methods available to them. The endeavor was a noble one on paper, a service to better the entire world. In practice, the benefits of her breakthroughs had been stolen from her again and again by her superiors.

Leda passed through the large glass foyer of the building, with its grand metal archways. She scanned her access card at the gates and was accepted inside. She no longer had any interest in contributing to the projects here. She'd developed a huge mass of material over the years, constructing impossible projects to meet her company's demands and establishing methods that revolutionized her field. But she would have access to none of that anymore. She remained, as ever, on little more than a standard employee contract even as her discoveries had truly enriched a handful of nameless individuals. Most of her superiors had forgotten she'd even created so many things.

Leda Palchek arrived at the elevators that would take her up to her workshop's level. Her laboratory was dedicated to analyzing everything available about the occasional spacecraft that passed through their solar system. The data was rarely conclusive, but simply knowing what was possible had driven her and her colleagues onward. Each day, they'd sharpened their models and improved the resolution on what they measured. They'd proven exactly which technologies had to exist. She was done trying to squeeze small, incremental improvements out of a system funneling all its discoveries into a classified database owned by a private consortium. She was ready for a higher level of thinking. Leda needed to leave behind the depressing mess the institutions of Vale Reach had devolved into and was genuinely grateful she'd found the chance to do so.

The elevator doors opened again, and Leda walked out into the main control room of the laboratory. The room was quiet and empty except for a thousand switches and dials. She was the first person to arrive that morning. No one wanted to face her on a day like today. They were concerned what she could potentially do on her way out. That thought pleased her slightly. She'd successfully applied for a program that would involve travel far away from Arkstone. She wasn't sure where exactly yet, potentially another continent, maybe within one of the decommissioned Sirkallion structures that still dotted the Vale Reach landscape. She'd been through an intense and competitive recruitment process and had only earned her place after signing a dense collection of strict confidentiality agreements. She would learn the details when her new project leaders determined it appropriate. As Leda thought back over the years spent working in this facility, she realized she'd never felt welcome within its corridors. She felt a sudden urge to leave. She accessed the building mainframe and disconnected her workspace from the building's reactor. The laboratory went silent at last. Leda was ready for bigger things.

*

The shuttle rattled under Cal. He'd seen enormous rockets on its exterior and could feel them preparing for ignition. The shuttlecraft was still on the launch pad. Along with around thirty other people inside, Cal sat facing upward. The interior of the shuttle was plain, with rows of seating in its narrow tube-like interior. Each person wore a harness of safety straps to hold them in place. At the front of the shuttle was a man a few years older than him, wearing the military uniform of Vale Reach and sitting facing them. He seemed highly alert.

They were going up to space, using a chemical rocket, not a space elevator. Cal had read how taxing it could be on the body. Cal turned to the person sitting next to him and pointed at the man at the front. "We're about to experience a lot of thrust. Is he going to be okay facing backward? It's no good for the eyes to accelerate backward."

"He looks like he knows what he's doing," she said. "I'd guess he's done this before."

As he looked around, he saw the range of ages in his fellow passengers. None were much beyond fifty, but none were younger than twenty either. He saw both security officers and civilians.

"My name's Cal," he told the woman next to him.

"Leda," she replied with a nod.

"Who are the rest of these guys?" he asked.

Leda replied with a list of names.

Cal nodded as though he understood.

"These must be the senior staff for the engineering division and the science division, wherever we're going, I expect," she said.

Cal considered whether he'd appear stupid for asking another question but did so anyway. "Engineering division for what? Where *are* we going? Other than away from Vale Reach, I mean."

"I don't know that"—Leda shook her head—"but we can't use a rocket like this to get very far from the planet."

"So the moon, then?" Cal asked in disbelief.

"Could be," Leda said.

Cal didn't have any idea what they'd be doing there. He knew of a few basic facilities on the lunar surface but nothing significant. Cal hadn't slept properly in two days, not since he'd first received the message. Stress was keeping him awake. Boarding a rapid flight across Vale Reach just to reach the launchpad here hadn't helped either. Something of massive significance was happening—historical. The officer at the front was definitely in a state of heightened tension, Cal thought.

The shuttle's engines grew significantly louder as they continued test firing in preparation for the quick push up to space. Cal's heart beat faster. He looked around again at the others on the shuttle. He recognized one of them, a cabinet minister from the global government. He thought he recognized some of the scientists too and began to consider what linked the people he recognized, what specialty they were all part of. The skills of the occupants onboard seemed beyond just the task of interstellar navigation that the document had described to him.

The security officer at the front reached out and pressed a button. "Please pay attention to the preflight briefing," he said as a video began to play on a large screen.

A man appeared. "My name is Garad Theeran, special coordinator with Vale Reach intelligence. Our world is in crisis," the man said. "It is likely we are reckoning with the gravest danger in our recorded history."

Sweat dripped from Cal's palms. A rocket launch was surely the most stressful way to get to space. The back of his throat felt as dry as a desert.

"As you may know, eighty-three years ago, our planet achieved independence under a series of treaties, collectively known as the Binding Treaty. It is under this agreement that we have lived, undisturbed, since that time. That era is now at an end. Our world faces annexation by the Universal Legion…"

Some of the people on the shuttle gasped loudly.

"And, under their terms, our status as a sovereign entity is due to end. This is not something we intend to allow," Theeran said. "You have all been selected as the crew of a starship that represents the future of Vale Reach. We must travel across much of the galaxy to arrive at the Ruarken High Senate. There, we will obtain the political guarantees that will secure our planet's future."

"Oh, hell," Cal murmured.

If the Binding Treaty was at an end, as the man claimed, life would forever change for the whole world.

"No one can know of our journey," Theeran continued on-screen. "Too many of our neighbors, such as the Sirkallions, want us to fail. Many of the planets ahead of us have already pledged their allegiance to the Universal Legion. Vale Reach must maintain the illusion of compliance with the Legion's demands, to not provoke them. We will leave behind the rest of our planet, and they must entrust us to protect their future. If Vale Reach falls under the dominion of an interstellar mercenary corporation, then the home we return to will be unrecognizable."

The man in the video appeared calm and confident as he delivered his speech. Cal looked over at Leda. She appeared to be grinding her teeth, her eyes almost bulging in fear. The shuttle continued to rattle violently, still moments before liftoff. The anticipation was unbearable.

"We don't know what lies ahead for us," Theeran said. "Neither can we predict what the Universal Legion has planned for Vale Reach. Yet we have obtained case files that indicate what they're capable of. Planet Vakri Argan, now used for disposal of unstable starship weapons. Planet Gok, mined for subterranean heavy metals until its continents collapsed. Planet Yadix, now the center of an orbital graveyard of derelict hulks awaiting deconstruction."

Facts and figures replaced Theeran on the screen.

"You all represent the best of Vale Reach. Today, we have assembled our brightest minds, along with our bravest and most committed soldiers. We have established a path that will lead us out of this darkness. To help us in this task, we have enlisted the help of a legal advisor, Advocate Fargas."

The screen changed to show an image of a man in a dark blue suit. *An offworlder.* Officially, none were supposed to be on Vale Reach.

"All of you are now part of a confidential mission until you are released from your duties. You will spend several years in space."

Cal froze in shock. No one else in the shuttle seemed as surprised as him.

"Our starship awaits us on the moon. We have created a vessel to carry us all the way to our final tribunal to secure the protection of our planet."

The shuttle launched, and the video shut down simultaneously. The roar of the engines and the powerful shaking overwhelmed Cal's senses.

When the shaking died down, Cal immediately felt loose in his seat. He floated fractionally above the chair. They no longer faced upward, as he no longer had any sense of up or down. Vale Reach lay far behind them, and they were drifting in space.

*

Rosco studied the occupants of the shuttle from his position at the front. They would have to learn to live and work together as a single unit. He prayed the selection process had been up to the task. Some looked nervous. It was understandable. Learning of the existential threat that faced them all was a sobering experience. The large screen activated again, now showing an image of a galaxy map.

"My name is Major Nurten Rosco," he said, "and I'm part of the security staff on the ship *Fidelity*. Welcome to our mission together. We are all vital parts of an indivisible team. The selection process has chosen you all for different reasons. Engineers, you are here to repair and upgrade the ship. Scientists, you are here to gather as much technical knowledge as possible to help strengthen our position. The security staff will escort you and protect you every step of the way. Diplomatic staff, such as our leader Councilor Theeran, you are the real reason we are here." He pointed at the display. "We must reach this location before our window to submit our petition to the Ruarken High Senate closes. If we can secure a guarantee of our protection soon enough, we will prevent the Universal Legion from beginning their operations on our world."

The map was daunting to look at, Rosco knew. It was also very vague and incomplete at the furthest reaches.

"Obviously, it's a long distance," he said. "The destination we're heading to is the Ruarken High Senate. It holds authority over approximately one quarter of the inhabited galaxy. Apparently, empires don't get much bigger than that. They are the only entity that is now willing to hear our appeal. All other institutions within range have rejected us already."

I'm the bearer of bad news. Best to get through it quickly.

"The diplomatic staff will file our petition in person at the public session of the High Senate. Obviously, the 'in person' part of that statement will be the most difficult aspect. The High Senate requires live testimony. Reaching the Ruarken High Senate will require forty-seven transit jumps for us. This process is estimated to take nearly two years. We have legal clearance for only approximately five percent of the route. The rest we will have to travel through covert means. In order to remain undetected, we will masquerade as a Palladian freighter, using fraudulent documents. Our ship, named *Fidelity*, must consistently maintain this illusion if we are to avoid being captured. We must be careful where we travel. It is everyone's responsibility to ensure our deception is successful."

The shuttle occupants looked ready, Rosco thought. Some even appeared resolute. That was a good sign. Every checkpoint would need to go according to plan, as they had so little margin for error.

"We have purchased Palladian visas and permits wherever possible. There are some backup plans and alternative routes factored into the system, but the schedule is tight. Instantaneous communication through the FTL lines to our home world will be available to us only at a very limited number of locations. FTL communication will require us to dock at facilities that are able to completely encrypt our transmissions. We do not anticipate there will be many of these. Once the journey begins, there will be no contact with Vale Reach until *Fidelity* reaches this system, the planet Aldethi."

The front screen changed to show a system much nearer their world but still many jumps away. Rosco added statistics of the ship's size and layout on the screen. He knew just how dangerous the mission would be. They would be alone, isolated, without allies. Normally, to bring civilians into that situation would be considered madness. Their ship lacked any shield generators. The weapons systems were close to negligible, only a few basic machine guns. Nearly all the reactor's power was needed by the engines to give their ship the maneuvering power equivalent to a Palladian freighter. Exterior panels for cosmetic purposes covered the structure of *Fidelity*, but against any kind of attack, they would provide no defense at all.

"It will be my job to keep the whole crew safe, along with fifty-nine more officers of the security staff and the expertise of over two hundred civilian staff, including yourselves," Rosco said. "Pirates will no doubt be a threat to us. Many could be mechanically modified with cybernetics. Some are even rumored to be mutated by alien toxins. We can't confirm the accuracy of these reports. Our initial major target is the Grand Highway of Thelmia, located here." He indicated another region on the map. "Reaching this checkpoint will mark the successful completion of the initial phase of our journey."

One of the scientists waved at Rosco, who tried to remember his name from the personnel files—Caladon, as he recalled. "What do we think is past that point?" the man asked.

Rosco paused for a second. He hadn't expected questions yet. "Beyond there, we have a few general ideas about what conditions in that part of space are like, but the region's largely unknown to us, other than the location of

Ruarken." Rosco knew the legends of outer space as well as anyone from Vale Reach did—tales of fearsome demons that devoured planets, and empires as old as time. "We'll likely obtain more data en-route to the Highway, which should allow us to minimize our exposure to hazards."

A woman seated next to Caladon raised a hand and also waved for Rosco's attention. "Will we be able to avoid time debt?" she asked.

Rosco had been hoping nobody would ask that question. He reached under his seat and pulled out a small envelope that was to be opened only in the event of being specifically asked about it. He took a sheet of paper from inside and cleared his throat. "Time debt is a theoretical phenomenon that is believed to affect all interstellar travel. As you may be aware, breaking the speed of light's limit is unachievable and technically cannot be done from a long-term perspective. Though ships appear to violate the speed of light when passing from one transit point to another, a starship can in fact only delay the results of challenging light. A metaphysical quantity known as time debt will be accrued by the ship with each successive faster-than-light jump. As further time debt develops, it becomes a burden on our ship, increasing the power requirements for the next FTL jump. This will add to the strain on the ship's reactor. If we do not have sufficient power when we attempt an FTL jump, we will be propelled into the future, by a minimum of years, potentially decades, or in severe cases, centuries. While our journey is anticipated to take two years for the ship and crew, if the mission sustains a severe setback, the time duration on the home world could be far longer." Rosco looked up from the paper. "Does that answer your question?"

"Wait, so you can't even tell us how long this journey will actually take for the people back home?" Caladon asked.

"If we keep to our schedule and stay ahead of time debt, the difference in time duration should be negligible. It'll need to be, or the mission will be jeopardized. If too much time is lost, our legal challenge won't be able to stop the Legion from establishing permanent control," said Rosco.

An uncomfortable silence settled over the room. Since the thruster had shut off, nothing else made any noise. Rosco thought of how close they were to the warships of Hardline Interstellar at that moment—maybe a hundred thousand kilometers away, no distance at all in terms of starship measurements. They'd likely been scanned already by the immense vessels. Their shuttle was part of regularly scheduled traffic to the moon base.

"*Fidelity* is capable of everything we require of it," Rosco reassured them. "It possesses all the essential systems of an interstellar starship, including maneuvering thrusters and artificial gravity. Much of our success will also be determined by our science and engineering divisions. The ship is equipped with cutting-edge research laboratories to interpret what we see. Once we leave the home system, the ship can receive data from the outside universe that Vale Reach hasn't accessed in decades."

"What do we tell people back home about what's happening?" Caladon asked.

Rosco shook his head. "You don't. Obviously, the release of this information is being tightly controlled on Vale Reach. We are due to arrive at the moon base in eighteen hours. There, you will each get the opportunity to make one call back home. The contents of your call will be strictly monitored to avoid the spread of confidential material. Advise your loved ones that you may be gone for at least two years. They will not hear from you again until we reach planet Aldethi."

*

In the far depths of space, Makron invasion armadas were docked at their harbors above the lightless and storm-wracked clouds of a dozen different worlds. Uncountable titanic vessels slumbered till the day they would be unleashed. Aboard each were ranks of Makron soldiers, waiting silently in dark vaults in cold storage, slurping slowly on their nutrient pipes. They had grown to be thick with muscle, enhanced by the rapid spin of their high-gravity ships. Custodian drones with thin bodies and long metal claws scurried over the machinery of the fleet, ensuring all systems functioned and all inhabitants were in optimal condition. Within the host were giants, muscles and bones swollen to vast size, each towering like a colossus in the holds, dreaming restlessly till the time they awoke to issue judgement and hammer a path through the Makron's enemies. Buried inside every Makron were the remains of a human being converted to the cause of the great empire. The entire ship pulsated with a single slow, deep heartbeat.

Beyond the line of control, warships of the Universal Legion patrolled the border of their territory. Constructed on a hundred different planets, these ships represented the units of countless different military divisions. The Legion was a conglomerate, a framework in which all member corporations would pull together toward a common purpose. They held back threats to humanity by any means necessary. Across ten thousand worlds, men and women labored voluntarily in the service of the Legion. Aboard the decks of the Legion's starships, uniformed officers maintained the machines and missiles capable of scouring life from every civilized world in existence.

Chapter 3

Cal was in a facility on the moon, with almost no gravity. He drifted back and forth inside a small cubicle, bouncing from one wall to the other while waiting for an answer on the phone.

Eevey answered the call. "Cal, how's the situation? Are you okay?"

Cal exhaled and shook his head. "Things aren't good. A lot's happening. Everything we suspected was correct."

"Damn," she said. "That not what I was hoping for."

"I'm going to be away on a long mission, maybe two years, they're saying. We're going out into space. I'm already in space now, actually. At the moon base—can you believe that?"

"That's incredible," she said. "But you're away for two years?"

"That's what it's going to be, apparently. Vale Reach could be facing a disaster. It feels like leaving you behind for two years is a disaster too. I goddamn hate this." He laughed bitterly for a moment. His eyes were filled with tears. "We can't even communicate for the first few months. No messages back home till we reach a safe point."

He couldn't see her face. Silence fell on the phone call as they struggled to find words. She sighed, a long and sad exhalation.

"I'm going to miss being with you," she said.

"I'll miss you so much," Cal said. That was a promise. The words were simple, but they felt binding. They would define his new outlook going forward. Regret and loss tangled like a knot inside his chest.

"I hate waiting," she said.

"Yeah, me too." They had that in common. He couldn't think of anything to say that could improve the situation. The sense of loss felt crushing to him. Cal sniffled loudly, trying to maintain some composure, and discovered how unpleasant his own mucus could be in zero gravity. "Are you going to be okay?"

"You should worry more about yourself," Eevey said. "You're going to need the help more than me."

"That could be true," said Cal. "It's going to be a dangerous road." He couldn't tell her just how dangerous it would be. He didn't want to torment her with dreadful details and spend this last conversation focused on the miserable odds against them. Eevey would figure everything out, he knew. No one could ever hide anything from her. Her mind was as sharp as a razor.

"What's your role on the ship?" she asked.

"I'll be producing the calculations that determine our approach vector to the transit points," said Cal. "There are a few others who could do it too, but I'm the one who invented the equations," he said. "They want me on the bridge to read the measurements as they come and to fine-tune any vector requirements. They're probably right that I'm the fastest at doing it."

"I suppose we should be glad they have you," she said after a moment's thought.

Cal smiled very slightly. "It sounds like our planet might be in need of a miracle. I think all of us are—you, me, everyone here."

He wished he could pace up and down in frustration, but his feet just wiggled above empty space as he tried to walk. The ship would have artificial gravity, at least, but he was already feeling drained and disorientated by his time away from the planet. He might never return to stand on the real earth of Vale Reach again. Cal was suddenly terrified. He didn't want to live without Eevey. They'd lived together in their apartment for nearly three years, and were engaged to be married. She was everything he had. Cal felt his life had finally started moving in a positive direction on the day he found her. She made him believe better things were possible. He owed her so much.

"When you come back," said Eevey, "we'll go for a walk along the shoreline. Then we can go to your favorite restaurant. We can go hiking in the forest or go to a festival with all of our friends. It'll be like nothing ever changed."

Cal smiled and looked down at the floor. When he'd left Eevey at the airport, neither of them had realized how long their separation would last. He couldn't imagine waiting two years before he'd be near her again.

"This is the best decision for everyone," Eevey told him.

"For everyone?" he asked.

"Yes, it is," she said. "Especially for everyone who isn't us. We benefit from it slightly less than everyone else."

"That's very true," said Cal.

"When you were a child, you always wanted to go to space and see all the other worlds," Eevey said.

He laughed nervously again. "Not quite like this. I think I envisaged something safer and a lot more convenient."

"Well, regardless, you got what you wanted," she said. "Maybe sometimes life not going according to plan is exactly what we need."

He let out a long breath. "How will I get by without wisdom like that?"

"I honestly don't know."

Cal tried to lean against the wall but bounced away from it again. He pressed his hands against his head. "Goddamn it. Why did this have to happen? I'm going to be so lonely." He was struggling to balance impulses of frustration and despair.

"Stay lonely," she told him. "That way, you'll understand exactly how I'm feeling."

Cal looked up at the ceiling. Or maybe it was the floor. "I do have to do this, don't I?" He had to ask a final time. He knew he was repeating himself.

"That's for you to decide," she told him.

"The answer is yes," he said. He felt distant as he said it. The logical part of himself answered the question. "It's definitely yes."

"Then go out there," she told him. "Go and do something great. I love you. You're brave. Just think, everyone in the world will owe you a debt even if they never know it. I'll be waiting for you on the other side."

*

The only things ever determined from the signals that came through Vale Reach's local transit points were the mass, length, and serial numbers of the ships and very little else. Cal had studied every case file exhaustively. He'd seen everything available to be seen, in terms of data.

He was silent with awe as he traveled with a group on an initial tour through *Fidelity*. He was seeing things he'd never imagined he would see. As no artificial gravity was operating yet, the group moved slowly and awkwardly with Rosco at the front. They examined everything around them.

"From this central hallway junction, we can access the laboratories, the engineers' workshops, and the reactor room," said Major Rosco. "Behind these hatchways here are access tunnels designed for maintenance and repairs on the ship. You're not encouraged to go into them unless you've got a clear understanding of what you're doing. Other exits from the junction head towards the exterior of the ship, where hardware such as our maneuvering engines and our suite of scanning tools are located."

Each of the crew had been issued a personal datapad upon boarding the ship. It was a flat, foldable screen that could be kept inside their uniforms, for accessing information at any time.

"Please examine the files I've now highlighted on your datapads," Rosco said as they continued to float along.

Cal saw a series of people's faces on the screen.

"These will be your superiors in each division, head scientist, chief engineer, our captain, security commander, etc. Please memorize them all." Rosco sounded distracted, as though those points were obvious.

The image of the captain showed a woman with gray streaks in her hair. Cal recognized her uniform insignia showing both the Vale Reach aerial and naval squadrons, and her name was given as Hekate Haran.

The group was nearing the end of the tour. Cal had a general understanding of the ship's layout. *Fidelity* was roughly ovoid in shape, and rotated around its central axis to provide a normal level of internal gravity. Its exterior was covered in a net of rigging made of metal cable, over which smooth sheets of polymer could slide into place, to provide a plow-like aerodynamic front face, should the craft enter a gaseous atmosphere at high speed. Sensors and probes covered its surface, yet Vale Reach had been careful to ensure that the aesthetics of the vessel closely resembled the Palladian freighter class they were imitating.

The ship's bridge was located in the spine of the ship, as far away from the exterior as possible. From there, all operations would be directed. Behind the bridge was the FTL drive, a mysterious spinning apparatus that was sealed away and that Cal did not begin to understand. Farther behind that was the reactor, a massive object that took up a significant portion of the ship's interior. The reactor would disintegrate heavy metal isotopes in its core and project the plasma out in a spray from the back of the ship. Finally, at the rear of the vessel was the main thruster array. Cal could see how tightly the whole ship fitted together. *Fidelity* had no space to spare onboard.

Cal raised his hand and waved to ask Major Rosco a question.

"Yes, Caladon," Rosco said without looking at him.

"I haven't noticed any escape pods during our tour through here. What is the procedure in the event of an emergency failure aboard the ship?" Cal asked.

Rosco looked at him and shook his head. "It has been judged that in an emergency, the safest action is for the crew to remain on the vessel. Therefore, currently, there is no evacuation procedure. Maintaining the integrity of the ship is our first and only option."

They continued down the corridor and passed the doorway that led to the reactor.

"What about the reactor? It can't be safe," said Cal. "It's extremely impressive, but I saw just how many experimental features it has. Throughout this whole ship, the crew compartments are interspersed with critical machinery. Has this all been properly thought through? If anything significant goes wrong, from either our own reactor or an external hull breach, we'll have almost no protection."

Rosco sighed. "Caladon, you'll be pleased to discover there is a suggestion box located somewhere on the bridge, where you can submit these concerns in writing. From there, they'll find their way to the proper channels. In the meantime, I can assure you that *Fidelity* has been built to the highest standards by the finest intellects available."

"The finest intellects available to Vale Reach," Cal responded.

"Operator Heit, at the end of this tour, you will be issued your uniform and rank badges, after which point you will have to refer to me as 'sir.' Are you aware of that?" Rosco asked.

"Right," said Cal. "Got it." He was too distracted by his many concerns over *Fidelity*'s design to play close attention to what Rosco was saying.

Rosco continued the tour. "Here we have our decontamination and air-scrubbing facility, which aims to limit the spread of any foreign pathogens that may colonize *Fidelity*'s systems. In particular, we have prepared a series of treatments that can counteract any carnivorous fungi that we encounter."

Cal's hands began to shake. The vessel was a death trap. Surely, he was only having a terrible nightmare.

Later that night, Cal lay in his small cabin bed. Across the back of a chair hung his uniform, red and white. Its colors were fresh and bright, even in the dim light of his cabin. He'd never imagined he would have to wear such a thing. It was a shock to his system, but the shock paled in comparison to learning of the devastation that awaited his planet if their mission failed. He looked at the steel walls and ceiling around him. He'd already begun his first night in the ship where he might spend the rest of his life. He would likely never escape it. The tiny cabin would be his only personal space until the day he was physically destroyed along with everyone else on this fragile, unsafe ship. *Fidelity* would stand no chance against even a single determined attacker. Any penetrating missile strike would rupture damn near everything. He imagined a rocket explosion within the crew decks. The searing fire bubble would burst outward. Cal felt his mind accelerating and tried to think of something calming to bring his anxiety under control. He concentrated his thoughts on Eevey. At least he would keep her safe if he could help keep Vale Reach safe. If he managed that, then meeting his doom in the narrow metal coffin around him would be worthwhile. Cal was willing to trade his life for hers. That was easier to say than to do, but he still felt sure it was true. No one ever wanted to put such an idea into practice, but his opportunity seemed to have come. History was made by people willing to lay down their lives, Cal told himself. It was important, vital work he was doing. He was saving a world. They all were. They just needed the goddamn ship to hold together.

Chapter 4

The warships remained at their stations in orbit high above Vale Reach. Their weapon systems were no longer on high alert but remained at the optimum position to strike. They could not be allowed to detect *Fidelity's* launch.

Fidelity was hidden securely in an enormous gas silo on the moon, a container just larger than the ship itself, supposedly built to store waste from Vale Reach's meager lunar mining operations. Vale Reach sold those waste gases to a roving chemical collector who wandered the void, buying cheap elements from isolated planets. In reality, Vale Reach had bribed the chemical collector with much of their remaining resources to provide a covert service, no questions asked. The collector was a rare interstellar visitor and one of the largest ships to visit, prior to the arrival of Interstellar Hardline. The privateer ships paid it no attention as it made its scheduled journey to Vale Reach's moon. The ship seemed colossal, but much of its structure was an empty frame in which chemical tanks could be collected and stored. As it passed by the Vale Reach lunar chemical plant, it dispatched clusters of small, single-man tugboat craft to obtain the canister on the moon's surface. These voidcraft flew spirals around the container, wrapping it in metal cables connected to the main collector ship. When their work was done, the cables were pulled back into the collector ship, and the gas canister, with *Fidelity* inside, was lifted up from Vale Reach's moon.

A full day passed as *Fidelity* waited whilst it was carried inside the slow gas collector. In the shadow of Vale Reach's largest planet, a rotund gas giant, the canister opened, and using small chemical maneuvering rockets, *Fidelity* slipped away from the collector ship. All officers were ready at their stations.

Leda Palchek felt more alert and focused than ever before in her life. The atmosphere on the bridge was electric. The artificial gravity produced by the ship's rotation was fully active. They were nearly a billion kilometers out from Vale Reach and still not yet moving under the power of the ship's main nuclear thruster. She was overjoyed that they'd successfully launched from inside the gas collector. The procedure began to fire up the main engine and bring the reactor to a high operational capacity. With a minor jolt that rattled the bridge, Leda felt the nuclear thruster come to life, and the ship accelerated. The internal forces experienced by the crew were small and constant, she noticed, but the sense of enhanced friction was welcome. Her arms were a little heavier, but she would adjust.

The bridge was cylindrical in shape, with a gently curved floor. Gravity on the bridge was directed outward from the ship's central axis, the same as throughout the rest of the ship. Being aligned with the rotational spine of *Fidelity* produced a line of zero gravity at the center of the bridge, and the crew's console stations and seating formed a continuous ring shape on the inside of the cylinder. Those on the bottom of the ring were upside down compared to those on the top side. Members of the crew sat ready in their seats, each held in place by a harness, with a desk of controls in front of them. During low-force maneuvers such as the ship was currently executing, the crew could easily leave their seats and walk around the bridge, but for the purposes of this test flight, they remained seated and secure. Beneath the bridge, the ship's operating systems were contained in several decks, connected to hardware in the ship's exterior. Much of the crew were stationed in those areas to direct and maintain the systems as needed.

Leda was seated at a desk on the bridge, somewhere behind the captain's podium. Her console displayed a holographic analysis of the Vale Reach system's transit points at the edge of the solar system. She knew only the basics of FTL travel. The ship would need to reach the transit point at a certain speed and angle in order to successfully make the jump to another point.

She looked at the rest of the bridge staff. Captain Haran's podium was near the middle of the bridge. Councilor Theeran was sitting with two advisors, observing. Many members of the science department were present on the bridge at that moment, as well as extra members of the engineering staff, ready in case any adjustments to the bridge's equipment were required. The rest of the engineers were either stationed throughout the ship to monitor the performance of *Fidelity*, or stationed in the workshop areas. The security officers were present, too, to study any incoming threats and to provide tactical analysis. At the front end of the bridge was a cone-shaped array of screens, its radius triple her own height, which presented a three-dimensional perspective showing all points of interest around the ship.

They were all witnesses to an extraordinary moment, Leda thought. *Fidelity* would complete the first successful transit jump in recorded history of a ship from independent Vale Reach. The ship's engines alone weren't enough to produce the speed they required for the jump. For that, they would pass through the gravity well of the largest planet in the system.

If they entered the transit point at the right speed, using the correct equations, they would translate to the next system with a velocity of one tenth the speed of light. They would remain at that high velocity—relative to their starting point—for the duration of their journey, probably years. All the transit points in the universe were deeply mysterious in origin, as far as anyone on Vale Reach understood. They were always found near the edges of solar systems, beyond the gravitational range of planets but usually in a plane with the planets' orbits. They connected to other transit points in neighboring solar systems, but no reason or pattern seemed to exist to explain which system would have many exits and which would have few. One common observation was that the transit points occurred almost exclusively in systems with human civilization, but which of the two had come first was an area of intense debate. Nobody knew if ancient humans had created the transit points or simply followed them.

"Captain, commence our initial acceleration maneuver," Councilor Theeran said.

"It's an honor to do so, Councilor," Captain Haran said. Haran opened a communication channel to the whole ship. "All decks, prepare for atmospheric descent and gravity-well acceleration."

Leda's console displayed to her the temperatures of the maneuvering engines that were arranged in rings around the exterior of the hull as they came to life to adjust the position and orientation of *Fidelity*. Across the front of the ship, the polymer cone stretched into place over the tip of the vessel to present a circular profile when they entered the deep planetary atmosphere. Leda realized her heart was beating quickly in anticipation.

She watched the huge screens as a speck of light in the darkness gradually expanded in their view to form an immense churning green sphere. No one from Vale Reach had ever seen another planet with their own eyes. It was like an orb, hypnotic and heavy with mystery. Something instinctive inside her failed to appreciate the scale of the object, almost wanting to deny what she was seeing. A human being was never meant to look at a whole world, let alone one as large as the giant she was currently looking at. They'd all get a close view of the planet during the acceleration maneuver as their ship raced across the thick inner layer of clouds and passed through the lighter skies above. As they approached the green sphere, it widened and flattened, shifting beneath them from a glowing disc to a wide horizon. Wisps of thin atmosphere curled around their vessel.

Leda felt they were contacting something unearthly. Though the ship was rotating, the screens displayed a stable image of the planet below them. The pull of the giant's gravity rapidly accelerated the ship, and Leda felt its force throughout her whole body. Across *Fidelity*'s exterior, the maneuvering engines intensified their rate of burn, correcting the ship's trajectory and holding them on course to pass over the storm's surface. The space outside the ship turned gray, the color of a sky. As the acceleration reached maximum, tension stretched her organs and blood vessels. The ship passed the point of closest approach, the numbers spinning by on the screens of the bridge. The acceleration forces reduced. *Fidelity* rose from the planet's atmosphere at its new higher speed. The sky outside the ship returned to the blackness of space. The green horizon ahead was restored to a vast orb that fell away beneath them. The forces Leda felt in her body returned to the minimal levels caused by the nuclear thruster. She checked the data on her screen. They had achieved the exact vector needed to jump across the transit point. She heard many of the bridge crew breathe a sigh of relief. Leda hadn't doubted the ship would pass its first test, but they'd reached a milestone nevertheless.

"Good work, Captain Haran," Councilor Theeran said with a smile.

Captain Haran showed quiet satisfaction. "Thank you, Councilor."

"Bring us into position for entry to the transit point. Open the channel to all decks again," Theeran said.

Captain Haran implemented the orders.

Theeran spoke up. "All crew, prepare to exit the Vale Reach home system. This will be last time we see the light of our own sun for several years. Today, we have crossed through the heavens that our people have watched powerlessly for generations. Now, we travel beyond that, to unknown stars."

At the far side of the transit point, their ship had a valid travel visa for the Palladian freighter they supposedly were. If they were caught traveling illegally, their vessel would get impounded, at a minimum. These matters of paperwork were important. From what Leda had heard, *Fidelity* would need every tool at its disposal if they were to protect their planet. Vale Reach was surrounded by people they couldn't trust, the Sirkallion Empire, Hardline Interstellar, even the Palladians, yet isolation had proven to be no defense. Leda examined the ship's records on what awaited them in the next system. Supposedly, their arrival point was filled with plenty of slow-moving traffic and planets sparsely populated and with limited development. *Fidelity* would blend in with the general flow of shipping in the star system. The crew were expecting only minimal presence from the kind of interstellar conglomerates that could potentially discover their fraudulent identity.

Leda watched the numbers that described the ship's position and speed, displayed on the screens around them all, counting down as they approached their target.

The transit point itself was invisible and approximately two feet in diameter, a cluster of exotic particles in a localized spot at the boundary of the solar system's heliosphere, just beyond the farthest planet. As they neared, the FTL drive was brought up to full power, the internal electric motors of its machinery creating a resonant hum audible throughout the bridge. Leda felt the hairs on her body rise as she imagined the imperceptible flux of strange energies radiating out from the hidden apparatus behind her. The response from her nerves could only be psychosomatic—it was impossible for her to actually feel the weak field it produced like a bubble to enclose the entire ship. When that spinning field collided with the particles of the transit point at high speed, a starship would somehow skip across space-time like a flat stone skimming a lake.

"All crew prepare for transit," Captain Haran said.

The moment had come. The maneuvering engines on the ship's exterior used their gas thrusters to minutely correct the ship's precisely chosen angle of approach. All systems were reporting full functionality. The ship's structures were well within mechanical tolerances. Conditions were ideal. Leda held on tight anyway.

In a minuscule fraction of a second, *Fidelity* crossed through the transit point and exited the Vale Reach system.

*

Major Rosco kept his gaze fixed on the main screen as *Fidelity* passed through the transit point. The crew had been advised they were unlikely to feel anything during the moment of transit itself. He didn't experience a change, but the systems of *Fidelity* erupted with data. A thousand radio signals flooded in from countless sources as they appeared instantaneously in a new solar system. Data rushed across the screens in a torrent. *Fidelity* was suddenly amongst the active traffic of a foreign star system. They had reached the rest of the universe.

Rosco looked around and studied how the crew were responding. He realized he hadn't fully anticipated what a sense of freedom they'd feel upon leaving Vale Reach. Many officers showed joy at their first successful transit, but others kept their attention fully fixed on their screens. They'd experienced a moment of relief, but they couldn't lose focus. They still had much work to do.

The solar system around them truly looked nothing like their own home system. Thirteen planets were there, four of them inhabited. Rosco saw two suns and eight populated moon colonies. Nearly two thousand registered starships were in the star system, far more than they'd expected. The new system was considered typical, according to records. Plenty of the systems ahead would be larger. More ships in the system could be both good and bad, Rosco knew. It would mean more potential encounters with enemies but also more of a crowd for them to hide amongst. The euphoria among the bridge crew seemed to die down as the seriousness of the task set in. *Fidelity*'s survival would require a combination of skill and luck.

Soon, a sleep-rotation system would begin, to ensure everyone aboard worked in shifts and had time off duty. The crew would begin their official duties. The engineering staff were tasked with assessing the capabilities of the starships and technology around them and using those findings to improve their own ship. The science department had a more abstract mission. Their stated task was to decrypt the hidden mysteries of the cosmos. When given the chance, they'd transmit that new knowledge back to Vale Reach.

For the time being, the goal was simpler. *Fidelity* simply had to reach the next transit point and continue its journey. The new system had three transit points, one of which they'd just entered from and two more leading away. Traffic flowed between the three, creating three streams of vessels. Occasionally, a ship would break off from its path to pass close by one of the planets or maybe to visit an asteroid cloud.

"Take us on a direct course to Transit Point Two," Captain Haran said from her seat on the captain's podium.

The pilot would control the ship's steering while they were in the midst of a traffic lane. He was kept isolated from the rest of the crew, in his own compartment at the nose cone of the ship. Rosco didn't know exactly why the man was kept separate, but many good reasons could exist. His brief discussion with the pilot during his initial arrival to the ship had made clear he harbored some secrets. Rosco suspected him to be another offworlder, just as Advocate Fargas was.

The simulated view of the space outside shifted as gas-powered engines along *Fidelity's* exterior rolled the tip of the ship to a new heading, realigning the vessel. The nuclear thruster shut down. Their ship had translated into the star system at close to the velocity required. No more adjustment of their speed was needed at the present time. The ship retracted its atmospheric deflection screens to better imitate the other ships around them.

Those unknown starships were gaining in clarity and shape as *Fidelity*'s systems worked to categorize the sprawl of radio signals bouncing throughout the star system. The ships grew from glowing dots on the screens to polygonal three-dimensional objects as *Fidelity's* own emitted scanning signals reflected back to them as minutes passed by.

Most ships were likely just passing straight through. Those would be bulk freighters, mostly carrying chemicals and probably very little crew. Their own vessel sought to imitate a smaller class of that type of ship. They traveled slowly on immense routes, often with no concern for the consequences of time debt.

The smaller starships in the system seemed to be moving between the passing freighters and the various planets and moon stations. Those worlds likely made much of their income delivering life-sustaining supplies to the interstellar traffic.

Rosco had to remain alert for any threats. He used his own datapad to assess a nearby ship, checking the ship's mass, half a million tons, and the infrared signatures across its surface. It was traveling at nine percent of light speed and likely had one full day remaining to complete its journey through the system. *Fidelity* detected no weapons systems. Its propulsion drives seemed modest relative to its bulk, and its thruster had already begun the process of gradually pushing the ship to the speed it required for its next transit jump at the system's edge.

Rosco turned his attention to the planets. Of those, at least, Vale Reach already had records. *Fidelity* would pass near none of them, which should ensure the planets posed no danger. In terms of their size and composition, they were as reported. It was hard for a planet to be out of place. Nearly every planet in the system had some kind of artificial facility in orbit, he saw. Rosco had reviewed the theories relating to the scale and requirements of orbital structures. Vale Reach had underestimated the quantity of refinery satellites around the gas giants. Three planets were inhabited on their surfaces, presumably with a full organic biosphere. The signals from those worlds were a tangled mess too dense to decipher. They plausibly held billions of lives.

"First watch officers, you are relieved from the bridge. You may exit your stations," one of the operations chiefs reported.

Rosco was free to leave his seat and move around the walkway areas. The auditorium-like structure of the bridge occupied forty meters of the ship's eight-hundred-meter length. When the bridge was operating on a standard level of manpower, the walkways between console stations would be mostly empty. He had already planned a jogging route that would take him around the entire interior of the ship with a minimal number of hatchways although running in an endless circle around the spine of the ship was another option.

Throughout the ship, people were preparing to begin the first day of their regular shifts aboard the vessel. Their entire existence would be organized by a set of carefully designed parameters. The ship absolutely depended on the physical and mental health of the crew. Its recreation areas were small, but spaces in the ship had been dedicated to giving the crew a place for their downtime. The canteen area would be where most crew socialized. Rosco had inspected every inch of *Fidelity* before most of the other crew had boarded. Not all the ship's systems had been active by then, though. The science labs and the machine workshops had been dark and dormant. They couldn't be fully tested until the ship could collect some useful samples from somewhere outside.

Something troubling appeared on the screen. Rosco experienced a nervous feeling. Their systems had detected the presence of many weapon energy signatures. Warships were clustered around the transit point they were heading to. A checkpoint was in place, operated by well-armed vessels all bearing similar military insignia. Vale Reach's analysis hadn't anticipated that level of scrutiny. The star system's inhabitants had significantly increased the rigor with which they checked passing ships. Rosco quickly searched for a solution using his datapad. The discovery of more military vessels was precisely what he'd been concerned about. The Universal Legion could be directing those ships if they were part of another contractor. Many of them carried high-powered laser weapons, able to attack their targets almost instantaneously. Rosco registered a ship with six gigantic lasers clearly visible, as well as two engines, each itself larger than *Fidelity*.

The largest vessels could be carrier ships, able to hold many squadrons of smaller voidcraft inside their hangar bays, such as gunships and bombers. Others appeared to be capital ships, potentially armed with devastating fission torpedoes. Given *Fidelity's* total lack of laser armaments, even one well-equipped hostile vessel could force an end to their expedition. The technology behind constructing gamma lasers was still entirely beyond Vale Reach. Military ships could possibly be outfitted with energy shield generators too, but those would be impossible to detect while inactive. Something seemed slightly chaotic about the ships' patrol patterns, he thought. They weren't properly organized. The serial numbers on the insignia suggested they were all only one part of a much larger fleet.

"We're receiving a message," one of the engineers reported. "One minute of delay on the transmission. It's from one of the military vessels."

There was uncertainty on the bridge. In terms of language, only a few crew members could converse directly with the offworlders. They had limited options for forming a reply.

"Connect them to the pilot's station. Let him talk to them," Advocate Fargas said to Captain Haran. "He'll know what they expect to hear. I'll listen in and make sure he sticks to our script."

Captain Haran gave him a curt nod then ordered the bridge crew to make it happen.

Listening on an earpiece, Fargas looked unhappy as he heard the message from the other ship. "We're dealing with a group called the Enforcers. I've heard of them. They ensure compliance with whatever laws are in place over the region." He paused for a moment to listen some more. "They're demanding an in-person inspection. They want to board us," Fargas said. "Marraz is just going along with everything, agreeing with whatever they have to say. I don't think we're suspected of anything in particular. They claim it's just a random inspection. They do this a lot. Although, in my experience, random inspections are never random. That's just a thing inspectors like to say."

"We can't allow any in-person inspection," Captain Haran said. "We'd be discovered as fraudulent immediately. They'd seize the ship and imprison us all." Captain Haran turned to address the rest of the bridge crew. "What are the options?"

Rosco watched on the bridge screens as one of the patrol ships latched onto a distant freighter in another part of the solar system. First, it used a series of grappling cables to make contact then launched a group of small boarding craft at its target.

"We should take an alternate route," said Rosco. "There's no way we can allow ourselves to get anywhere near those military ships."

"What is through the other transit point, Major?" Councilor Theeran asked.

The third transit point in the system had the least traffic of all and no checkpoint.

"Our navigator will know that," Rosco said.

Operator Caladon spoke up. "Allumia. That's where it will take us."

Captain Haran seemed unimpressed. "How far will Allumia take us off our initial route?"

"It should be just a few weeks overall loss to our journey time," Caladon said. "From Allumia, we'll go to Paxis and then from Paxis to Eerdul, and then we're back on track. The Allumia system is supposedly empty, sir. No major settlements reported—generally, no interstellar traffic."

Captain Haran and Councilor Theeran consulted quietly with each other for a moment, forming a mutual decision.

"All right," Theeran said after a second of consideration. "Change lanes. Bring *Fidelity* to the Allumia transit point. We'll go to an empty system instead of risking these inspections."

The bridge suddenly came alive with activity as all personnel hurried to implement the orders. The crew experienced a light pull as the maneuvering engines quickly repositioned their ship, followed by the push of the nuclear thruster accelerating them to achieve a new vector.

"One of the Enforcers' ships has now aligned its sensors in our direction," a member of the bridge crew reported.

"It's warming up its engines," another engineer said—Leda Palchek, Rosco remembered. "It could be preparing to come after us."

"Get us out of here first," Captain Haran said.

It should work. Rosco studied the Enforcers' ships again in apprehension. It would have to work.

The crew kept careful watch on the checkpoint's warships as *Fidelity* approached the transit point to Allumia. The ship that had scanned them left its position and approached them, but *Fidelity* made physical contact with the mysterious transit point and vanished from the system.

Chapter 5

The electronic hubbub of the bridge quieted immediately after the second transit, Cal observed. The chatter and alerts of the previous system's radio signals had become a continuous murmur without him realizing. Once again, they were plunged into a silent star system.

"Scan the planets," Captain Haran ordered.

A list of worlds filled the main screen, thirteen to be precise. But something more was there, a starship, immense and dead. Cal applied a series of filters to the data, rapidly developing his analysis. It was cold, the temperature of the vacuum, incapable of sustaining life. Gargantuan in length and covered with great tears and gashes, the object was so large that Cal initially mistook it for an asteroid. *Fidelity* kept its distance while learning what it could. Isotope signatures indicated the ship was at least three-and-a-half millennia old. There was virtually no chance it contained anything of value. Over time, raiders would have picked it clean till only its skeletal carcass remained. Despite its unimaginable age, the signs of war could still be seen across its surface, where the ancient scars of laser battles and explosive strikes were cut into the metal. Twisted ruptures in the hull burst out like razor-sharp flowers, frozen for eternity. It remained silent and enigmatic, the relic of another age. *Fidelity* turned its attention to the system's planets.

The planets, too, offered a surprise. One stood out in particular. Cal noticed all the other scientists and engineers on the bridge studying the same one that caught his attention.

"Report on the planets," Captain Haran ordered.

"One of them is exceptional." Leda sounded filled with awe, and some of the bridge staff turned to look at her. "It's…" She struggled for the right word. "Spectacular," she came up with.

"Engineer Palchek, what are you talking about?" Haran asked.

"The upper section of the atmosphere is filled with complex nitrates. They seem to naturally separate into thick layers, like a fractional distillation amongst the clouds. According to our sensors, the lower sections contain plenty of combustible hydrocarbons, maybe with phosphorous and sulfur on the surface below. It's valuable. Very valuable. If we collect samples, maybe even stock up on as much as we can, we could potentially synthesize some superior chemical fuels for our maneuvering engines…" Leda looked uncomfortable, realizing she'd spoken more than normal.

"Stock up?" Councilor Theeran asked her.

Captain Haran answered him. "Obviously, when *Fidelity* set out from Vale Reach, we made sure the ship was supplied with the most powerful fuel we could obtain. But…" Haran paused for a moment as she studied the data on the screen. "There might be chemicals down on this planet that we just didn't have access to."

Cal agreed with Leda's assessment and spoke up. "If we can extract material from the atmosphere of that planet, it could contain compounds with attributes that'll enhance our ship's capabilities."

"What are the risks?" Councilor Theeran asked the bridge crew.

"The atmosphere is turbulent. It's hard to predict what state it could be in, lower down," Leda said. "None of our scanning tools can penetrate far, sir."

"We cannot risk the safety of the ship," Councilor Theeran said.

"It's likely that we wouldn't even need to go very deep to obtain the most powerful fuel that our equipment could handle," Cal said. "There may be superior fuels even deeper inside, but there's a limit to the heat we can put through the maneuvering engines anyway."

"We can flood the shuttle deck with atmosphere, then crew can go in with void suits and fill our gas tanks. Our ship wouldn't need to enter the more hazardous areas," Leda said.

Theeran looked back up at the main screen. "Do it slowly," he said.

Captain Haran nodded. "Operations, bring us within ninety kilometers of the surface of Allumia Eight. Engage the atmospheric deflectors."

*

Fidelity crossed the quiet space of the Allumia system, approaching Allumia Eight. Cal watched the planet grow in detail on their screens, white and blue in their vision, with murky skies that gave no hint of the surface below.

Across the front exterior of the ship, the rubber shielding panels returned to their position over the tip of the vessel. They were about to be tested more severely than before. Everyone on the bridge instinctively took hold of something solid as the ship dipped into the atmosphere like a swimmer slipping below the surface of the water.

The screens aboard the bridge darkened as thick clouds obscured them.

"I want maximum power on the external hull lights," Captain Haran said. A few beams of white light thrust out into the opaque, swirling blue soup they were immersed in.

Cal sat up in shock, suddenly alert. "Captain! We're picking up a signal from the surface below. *Fidelity* couldn't detect it before now, but it's reaching us since we moved below the cloud canopy," he said, reading the data on his screen.

"What is this signal?" Haran demanded.

"It sounds like a weak call that's being constantly broadcast. I'm trying to get more detail," he said. "Likely, the signal didn't have enough power to penetrate these clouds. This transmission's likely inaudible to anyone who isn't already inside the planet's layers."

"It's a distress signal," said Leda. "Definitely coming from ground level."

The ship trembled very fractionally from the thick, almost liquid atmosphere washing over the surface outside.

"A distress signal? How can we be sure of that?" Rosco asked.

"It's too weak to carry any kind of audio, but it's pulsating. It's tapping out a code," Cal said. "I've seen it before in a database of common codes that Vale Reach assembled over the years. It's a universal signal for someone in need of rescue, but it's a much older type, almost archaic."

Theeran considered the situation for a moment. "Senior officers, retire to the conference room," he said.

Haran, Theeran, and Fargas, plus Major Rosco and several others, left their positions and exited down a small stairwell, leaving *Fidelity* in control of the bridge crew. Cal exhaled in frustration as he simply awaited their decision.

*

"Do we know anything about who could be down there?" Councilor Theeran asked. "Anything at all?"

The conference room was silent. No one had an answer.

"There would be no reason to intentionally send a signal that weak," Rosco said. "It's pointless. So whoever's down there must be very low on power and probably conserving what they have left. Potentially, they could have been there a long time, given that we've found the signal only by accident. We don't even know if they're alive. It could be an automated signal at this point…"

"It's probably for the best if whoever's down there has less power remaining than we do. That's an advantage for us," Advocate Fargas said.

"There is the possibility that whoever's down here may have seen us already," Rosco said, "depending on what their own scanning capabilities are."

Theeran turned to the blue-suited offworlder. "Is it legal for us to collect this gas, Fargas?"

"This star system has been reported as abandoned. As an unclaimed space, the mineral rights belong to no one at the present time," the man replied, his head bobbing slightly.

Theeran nodded. "And do we have any legal obligation to investigate this distress signal?"

Fargas shrugged. "Depends exactly on what jurisdiction we think we're under. If we're ever questioned, I could get us out of trouble, either way."

Theeran sighed in what seemed like deep frustration. "I do not like risking the entire ship for a diversion."

"We can send a shuttle down to investigate the surface and keep *Fidelity* far away in the upper reaches of the atmosphere, where it's safe, while we attempt to extract the fuel from the storms as Engineer Palchek described," Captain Haran said.

Theeran nodded after a moment of consideration. "That could work."

"There's a problem, with all due respect, sir," Rosco said. "We've already discussed how volatile the lower atmosphere is. How can we send a shuttle to the surface without significant risk?"

Captain Haran thought for a moment and turned to address Advocate Theeran. "We do have someone who could get the shuttle down to the surface," she said to him.

Theeran seemed surprised. "We're going to risk him on this expedition?"

"If anyone can get down to the surface, it's him. Our best chance of success is to give the pilot control of the shuttle," Captain Haran said.

"Can we be sure he will even bring the shuttle back to us?" Theeran asked. He seemed to be joking, but no doubt he was indicating a real concern.

Haran nodded to Rosco. "Rosco, you can keep him under control. Maintain discipline on the shuttle."

Rosco wasn't expecting that at all. He nodded, ready to comply.

"If we pull this off," Advocate Theeran said, "we can claim salvage rights on whatever's down there. It may not be much, but getting our hands on any hardware from beyond Vale Reach would allow you to start improving the ship's systems immediately. I'm sure your engineers might even have a chance of replicating some of what they see."

There was a moment of intense consideration.

Theeran looked over at Captain Haran again. "Are we sure the pilot can safely do this?"

"No doubt he certainly thinks he can," Haran muttered.

Theeran smiled. "Prep a shuttle to go down to the planet surface," he said. "But order them to withdraw at the first sign of trouble."

"Major Rosco, assemble an eight-man security team," Captain Haran said. "Bring a few engineers with you to ensure the shuttle stays within safe operational limits and to assess whatever's down there. Discover the source of the signal."

*

Cal was sitting in the cafeteria of *Fidelity*. It had a low ceiling, part of a narrow space within the outer decks. On one side was a large message board where the crew could leave notes for each other, plus a screen that displayed briefing messages from the captain. The walls were metal but painted white, with photographs of the landscapes and cities of Vale Reach. The room's capacity was fifty people, but between the ship's mealtimes, it became mostly empty. Cal felt apprehensive. He was sitting in a wooden chair at a round table, counting down the minutes until his next shift began, when Major Rosco walked in and approached the counter for food. Cal watched him for a few minutes as he chose his meal.

"Hey! Hey, Major Rosco, hey!" Cal waved to him.

Rosco came over. "Operator Heit, how are you today?"

"Good," said Cal. "Let's sit. Have a chat. Let's compare notes. And you can call me Caladon. Or Cal."

Rosco looked around the room quickly, as though searching for someone. He shook his head and sat at Cal's table.

"How are you finding bridge operations?" Cal asked him.

Rosco laughed in surprise. "Fine."

"Are my services as navigator satisfactory?" Cal asked him.

"We've only done two jumps so far," said Rosco. "But, yes, I'd say we've all achieved what we're looking for so far. Your navigation work has been excellent."

"How about that pilot?" said Cal. "I calculate the vectors, but he has to line us up and deliver them. What's he like?"

"Yeah," someone said.

Cal and Rosco both looked round to see Leda at a table behind them.

"What is up with the pilot?" She got up from her seat and came over to join them.

"Nothing is up with the pilot," Rosco said.

"Then why aren't we allowed to see them?" Leda asked.

Rosco rolled his eyes like he was dealing with children. "Because our superior officers have deemed that his identity should remain classified."

"So it's a 'he'?" Leda asked. "You're confirming that the pilot is male?"

"And that just one man does it all? But something about him needs to be classified?" Cal added.

Rosco sat in bewilderment for a moment, looking at them both. They stared at him as though they expected him to continue.

"I cannot share classified information with you." He got up and went to another table.

Cal and Leda watched him walk away.

"He nearly let out something interesting there. I reckon we can get more from him if we keep trying," Cal said.

"Perhaps," Leda said. "It's his job to not spill any secrets. That is the general point of the military." She smiled. "But perhaps we can make it happen."

"Technically, this isn't a military ship," Cal said. "It's controlled by the civilian government."

"Technically," Leda said with a small smile. "But I think when most of our top ranks are military, it becomes a military ship."

"They're only a third of the crew. Do you think they're here to keep an eye on us?"

"No doubt."

Cal sighed. His heart suddenly felt heavy, he realized. He missed Eevey. The feeling came to him at unpredictable times. He felt like his relationship with her was already history. He found it hard to believe that a return to normalcy would ever be possible.

"Are you glad you joined this mission?" he asked Leda. He didn't know what sort of answer he wanted to hear.

"I am," she said without much hesitation. "We're exploring a new, unknown planet. Or exploring the upper atmosphere of a new planet, at least. That's not at all how I thought my life would go, just a few weeks ago."

Cal leaned forward as he thought about that and realized she had a point. "That is pretty great, isn't it? We're about to be exploring a new planet." He laughed slightly. "And I never dreamed I would be. Maybe life doesn't get much better than that."

"I would have traded anything to come here," Leda said, "especially if I'd known what this mission involved."

"I did trade a lot," Cal said. "I miss what I left behind. Every so often, I'm not sure I made the right choice."

"Exploring new worlds isn't enough for you?"

"Not when it comes at the expense of what I love most about my old life."

"Maybe you'd change your mind if you experienced the new world in person," Leda said.

"You think I would?" said Cal. "I wasn't planning on going into any hostile environments."

"Are you really going to pass on the chance to feel another planet under your feet?" She seemed animated, enthralled by it.

He considered the idea. "I'd be a fool to miss that."

"Then come to the shuttle bay. They're assembling a special crew to reach the surface."

Cal shook his head. "Too dangerous."

"Then you'll lose out on the only benefit to being here."

Countless generations of people from Vale Reach had dreamed of such a moment. As Cal imagined his terrestrial-bound ancestors and their yearning for space, he found it harder to ignore their collective wisdom.

"You've convinced me. I should venture outside the ship."

*

Leda arrived with Cal in the hangar bay.

"You know what you're doing, right?" Major Rosco asked them as they climbed onboard a shuttlecraft being prepared for launch.

The interior of the shuttle was dark and made cramped by the dozen or so people already inside.

"Of course I do," Leda replied.

Cal just nodded.

Rosco seemed concerned for a moment but then turned away to address something else.

Equipment was being loaded onto the craft by the crew stationed in the hangar bay—pressurized void suits, survival kits, and other heavy crates Leda didn't recognize. A mix of security officers and engineers comprised the team journeying to the planet below. The soldiers all carried automatic rifles, the kind she'd seen on Vale Reach.

A loud, mechanical whine sounded as the door sealed shut. Red lighting in the shuttle's interior came on and Leda saw everyone taking their places in the rows of seating. She hurried to an empty chair and strapped herself in.

For several minutes, they waited as the shuttle crew conducted their last preflight checks. Then the bay doors in *Fidelity* beneath the shuttle burst open, and the shuttle was thrown into the storm outside. Leda shut her eyes tight and held on with a white-knuckle grip as the pilot stabilized the shuttle craft and, after a few moments, brought it under steady control. The shuttle rattled alarmingly, but they were no longer being shaken wildly around. Leda looked up, and for a moment, she glimpsed a man she didn't recognize at the controls, with bright metallic hair.

Rosco leaned over to talk to him. "Nicely done. You almost made it feel easy."

"It wasn't," the silver-haired man told Rosco.

"Bring us down slowly toward the signal," Rosco said.

"Twenty minutes," he said.

*

The shuttle set down on a rocky surface. Its small metal legs extended to grip the ground. The crew felt the strong natural gravity of the planet rather than the calibrated artificial spin gravity of *Fidelity*. Everything was far heavier than expected. Rosco's body was instinctively confused. The only experience he could compare it to was climbing a mountain with a heavy backpack, his muscles constantly lifting weight.

Everyone onboard equipped themselves with a plastic hood and a rebreather mask, as well as thick gloves to cover their skin and insulate their temperature. Each wore a thick outer coat that added to their weight. The security officers checked each other and the civilians to ensure they were fitted properly. Analysis from *Fidelity* indicated that the conditions outside could be tolerated for at least several hours if they wrapped up. Rosco confirmed everyone was prepared for the change in atmosphere, including Marraz, who still sat at the shuttle's controls. Rosco had already withdrawn the ignition keycard that would allow anyone to operate the engines, keeping it secure on his person.

"Opening the shuttle," Rosco announced.

The bolts sealing the door withdrew with a mechanical whirring, which seemed deafening. His heart raced. The door slid away from the frame with a pop, and the two atmospheres combined. Some of the crew gasped as the door continued to lower, revealing a foggy landscape of bare rock. Visibility was low, but Rosco could see for at least two hundred meters along the side of a huge mountain range ahead of them. Another planet. He took the initiative and stepped out the door and down the ramp. As he emerged outside, he felt a thrill at experiencing the strange alien daylight. It was a radical transition from the electric confines of *Fidelity*.

"Squad, take your positions behind me," he ordered.

The rock beneath him was cold, hard, and sharp, and the low temperature of the air reached quickly through his many layers of clothes. The rest of the crew followed behind him in an arrowhead shape, a group of fourteen overall.

Rosco looked down at the scanning device in his hand. He was leading them toward the source of the signal. The mountainside became steep, and the group formed into a narrow line to travel safely. Rosco looked with concern at the deep drops into the murky depths that surrounded them on many sides, as well as the layer of loose sand and gravel at the edge of each precipice and crevasse. They had to press ahead. Turning back to the ship without any results and offering Captain Haran nothing was not an option.

He walked around the side of a large round hill and saw what he was looking for. A crashed spaceship was crumpled into a mountainside. It stretched out of sight into the fog, obscuring its true length. Potentially, it was equal in size to *Fidelity* though the crash had deformed the ship significantly. Two figures were there, wearing black, standing and watching them—waiting for them, it seemed. The figures were tall, with large hoods over their faces. Rosco stopped walking. The hooded figures made no movement. He watched them warily. The rest of the group abruptly came to a stop behind him. After a moment, one of the distant figures raised a hand in greeting.

Rosco turned back to the rest of the group. "Let's go meet them. Keep your weapons lowered."

They continued along the mountainside path. As they neared the crashed ship, Rosco noticed that the two figures wore some kind of loose jumpsuit, seemingly of black leather, which was tucked into their boots at the bottom. No faces were visible. The crashed spaceship was an eerie thing. What remained of it was nearly eighty meters in diameter, Rosco estimated, though much of it had collapsed. Its exterior was so scraped and worn that its features were unrecognizable, yet the intact half seemed occupied. He reasoned that the two figures likely sheltered in the wreckage.

The narrow path they traveled along reached a wider plateau on which the crashed spaceship lay. Rosco's sense of vertigo was replaced by apprehension toward the two figures. The crashed ship's occupants were just meters away at that point. Both were facing him directly. He waved at them in greeting but felt unsure what to say. Rosco realized that *Fidelity* had perhaps sent the wrong person for the job.

"Hello," he settled on. He waited for a response.

One of the black-robed people said something Rosco didn't understand. The voice was masculine. Then the person turned and said something to their compatriot.

Rosco decided not to ask about the status of their vessel since the answer was obvious. "Your spaceship has crashed here," he said. That, too, was an obvious statement, he realized.

The black-robed man again said something Rosco couldn't make sense of.

"I don't understand you, unfortunately," Rosco said. He pointed toward the rest of the group. "We are from a nearby starship. We are in orbit above you." He spoke slowly, hoping it would make a difference.

"I see. I think I have determined the key elements of your language," the man said.

"I understood that!" Rosco said, nodding with enthusiasm.

"Yes, something from the Sirkallion region. Quite fascinating," the man said.

Rosco shook his head at the mention of Vale Reach's old rulers. "I am Major Rosco, the leader of this expedition." He gestured toward the rest of the group again.

"I am Cartographer Yendos. This is my assistant, Ontu. And yes, our ship has crashed." The man was extremely tall and very broad too, like a monolith.

"Have you been here for long?" Rosco asked.

"Yes," Yendos said. An awkward silence settled over the group. "Would you like to come into what remains of our ship?" he asked.

Rosco looked around, taking in the foggy mountainside. "Let's do that."

Chapter 6

The ship was on its side, which turned its original decks into steep, diagonal surfaces rising high above the crew like a cliff face. Conversely, the sections of the ship that had impacted with the ground were the easiest to walk on. In places, the bare rock of Allumia Eight was exposed beneath their feet. The group initially arrived in some large holding area within the ship, which wasn't fully sealed from the exterior atmosphere.

Leda was pleased to see that the ship used rotational gravity, with decks arranged around its center, exactly the same as theirs. That matched the understanding on Vale Reach that any ship with artificial gravity would use rotation. The ship's reactor was definitely dead, so the interior was pitch-black except for the electric torches carried by the crew. Yendos himself had a powerful light attached to his hood.

"Many decks were breached in the initial crash landing," Yendos said. "We attempted to set down on the plateau, but we collided very hard with the mountainside here."

Leda took note of how open and spacious the inside of the ship was. They had successfully miniaturized many systems for extra efficiency.

"How many were your original crew?" she asked as they walked along through its interior.

The other offworlder turned to face her, the one referred to as Ontu. "There were seven of us, originally. Only Yendos and I survived the crash."

"Oh. I'm sorry," Leda said.

"It was a difficult time for us," Ontu said.

The cold seeping in through Leda's clothes made her feel numb and drained. Entering the vessel hadn't done much to help the temperature situation. The air was as cold within the ship as outside.

Yendos was walking ahead with Rosco but suddenly stopped. "Much of the rest of the ship beyond here is in a state of hazardous disrepair. Perhaps you would be best served by making yourself comfortable in this area?" Yendos snapped his fingers, and his assistant hurried over to a metal cylinder in the center of the chamber. Ontu turned some kind of wheel, and a hiss of gas was followed by the roar of a bright orange flame bursting to life.

Leda instinctively took several steps toward the heat. The rest of the engineers moved with her. Even the security officers subtly drifted nearer the large gas fire.

Rosco looked around and nodded. He didn't have a clue what he was doing, Leda realized.

"Okay," Rosco said. "This seems fine. We should introduce ourselves properly. But first, are you in any immediate danger? We received a distress call from you although it was very faint."

Yendos put his hands together. "We are greatly improved now you are here, no doubt. We are in need of transport away from this cursed rock. We have been marooned for nearly three standard years now. I pray for nothing more than for our ordeal to be at an end."

Leda wished she could see the man's face, but the large leathery hood covering his head was totally opaque and sealed up at the front. The soft, plastic hoods the *Fidelity* crew wore were transparent, except for the mist of their own breath.

"That's…" Rosco hesitated. "That's possible. We should be able to manage that."

"Wonderful," he said. "You said you had a much larger ship in orbit?"

"Yes," Rosco said. "Perhaps I should call down a representative to discuss your travel arrangements?"

Yendos patted him on the shoulder. "That would be best. Please, invite them down." Yendos turned and walked away into the shadows, with Ontu following.

"Where are you going?" Rosco asked.

Yendos turned back. "We must gather our few remaining possessions, ready for the journey away from here. Please, enjoy the flame."

He vanished out of sight.

*

Rosco watched *Fidelity*'s engineers drag a series of small metal crates from inside the dead ship toward the burning gas canisters as seating. Some removed their gloves to help the flame warm their fingers more quickly. The security officers all remained on their feet and alert.

Rosco knew they had no reason to trust the occupants of this ship. He looked around. The metal walls had exposed piping and rapidly disappeared into the darkness. He had no idea what he was looking at. He wished he could make sense of it and gain some insight into what was going on. He was responsible for preventing anything jeopardizing *Fidelity* or its crew. He feared he'd already said too much, but he couldn't exactly deny they had a ship in orbit.

He sat down next to Leda on one of the crates. Cal was nearby.

"What do you make of this place?" Rosco asked her.

"It's fantastic," she said. "A little grimy, and it's obviously crashed into a mountain, but it's incredible. There's so much to take in. I always tried to imagine something like this, an advanced-technology starship. It's a whole different experience to seeing *Fidelity*. This ship was built by people who really knew what they were doing. Not to insult the engineers of Vale Reach, but…" Leda shrugged.

"Did you see any weapons systems? Back when we were outside or in here?"

"No. Nothing that looked like a laser or a railgun. They might have torpedo tubes inside. Hard to tell," Leda continued. "These gas canisters are the main thing I see in here. Extracting hydrocarbons from the atmosphere is clearly no problem for them. Fuel gas is probably the one thing they do have. How are our own efforts going aboard *Fidelity* to collect chemical fuel from the storm?"

"Apparently, they're making good progress," Rosco said. "What do you make of the crew here?"

Leda thought for a second.

"They seem weird," said Cal. He leaned in to join the conversation. "We haven't even seen their faces yet. But I don't want to be judgmental. They're the first offworlders we've met. Do you think all offworlders are like that?"

"I guess I don't know," Rosco said.

"I don't think we can leave them here," Leda said.

"No?" said Rosco.

"They've been waiting three years for rescue. Their ship's almost fully out of power. It doesn't have the energy to transmit their distress beacon beyond this heavy atmosphere. If we don't get them out of here, I'm not sure anyone will."

Rosco nodded his head and looked at the floor. "That's very humanitarian of you."

"Well," Leda said, "if we tell them we're leaving them behind, they're going to take it pretty poorly. I know I would. Then we may really have a problem on our hands."

Rosco let out a long sigh.

"She's right," Cal said.

"What do we do next, Major?" Leda asked Rosco.

"Fortunately," he said, "we aren't the ones who decide that."

*

The shuttle descended through the stratospheric typhoon once again, carrying Councilor Theeran from *Fidelity* to the surface. It plunged through the clouds and returned to the rocky plateau. The security crew brought Theeran indoors to what remained of the crashed ship.

"What brought you to this area?" Theeran asked Yendos.

They were both in a small side room, as lightless as the rest of the wreck, where another burning gas cylinder provided heat. Theeran had removed his own breathing mask, but Yendos made no move to remove his hood.

"We are explorers, members of a cartography guild. Our path is to catalogue and record the terrain of the universe," Yendos said.

"That sounds very fulfilling," Theeran said. "I apologize if this sounds insensitive, but who funds these expeditions?"

"We sell our data privately, to finance our continued journeys," Yendos said. "What brought your ship to this area? It is, unfortunately for us, a rarely visited corner of space."

Theeran hesitated, but he had his answer prepared. "We're traveling to consult with advisors on a distant planet. It's a long journey."

Yendos shifted in interest. "A long journey, you say? Those are a specialty of mine."

Theeran smiled at him in a reserved fashion. "What happened to your ship?"

"Our ship entered below the cloud canopy of this world to map the mineral flows in this turbulent atmosphere, but engine failure forced us to land abruptly. We fractured our reactor when we suffered a collision."

A moment of awkward silence passed between them.

"Let me offer a token of my good will," Yendos said. "During my investigation of this region, I discovered several unmarked transit-point vectors. There were no accurate records of these routes before my surveys."

Theeran almost laughed. "You know how to offer someone what they want to hear."

"I'm quite sincere," Yendos said. He produced a black datapad from within his robes and passed it to Theeran.

Theeran looked at the device for a second then put it in a pocket of his insulated coat. "Suppose we were to allow you aboard our ship. We have many highly sensitive documents and materials in our possession, including the design of the ship itself. You would have to agree to avoid restricted areas onboard and make no attempt to view any of our classified content."

"Done," Yendos said. "I have no interest in bureaucracy."

"I also have to advise you that our living quarters are somewhat bare and functional in design. Your accommodation on our vessel may not be at a standard you are used to although…" Theeran took in the ruined state of the ship around them.

"My assistant and I will manage fine with whatever conditions are available," Yendos told him. "Might I now, Councilor Theeran, inform you of what I may do for you?"

"Go on," Theeran said.

"I note, and I pray you take no offence, the unique dialect your people use. Quite beautiful, but not widely understood. May I assume, from the nature of the people sent to greet me, that you lack an interpreter?"

Theeran shook his head. Fargas had language skills. "We have someone for that, but he stays on the bridge."

Yendos shook his head in disagreement. "They will be hard-pressed to match my range. It is one skill among many that I've developed from a lifetime of traveling so widely. Let me propose an agreement between us. In return for food and lodgings aboard your ship until you reach a planet that I deem of sufficient interest for me to explore, I will share with you the knowledge and expertise I have gathered from nearly two centuries of journeying. As a data merchant, I assure you, I have a total understanding of discretion."

"You're asking to join us until you can reach another planet to explore?" Theeran studied the faceless black hood.

"I'm asking not to be left behind here," Yendos said slowly.

"Sounds like you're offering us a good deal," Theeran said after a moment.

"Then we are shipmates. It's settled." Yendos stood up. "Councilor Theeran, you are a credit to your people. Now, I believe my assistant Ontu is nearly done stripping what remains of value on this ship. As another token of my gratitude, I'm sure we can offer some spare parts."

*

The shuttle rattled aggressively as it climbed up through the skies once again. Cal and Leda were aboard, seated at the rear with the other civilians on the trip. Sitting adjacent were Yendos and Ontu, strapped into the seats of the shuttlecraft just like everyone else. Cal thought they looked uncomfortable. The two of them were far larger than the seats were designed for. Their black hoods still covered their faces. Cal wondered if they surveyed their surroundings with disdain or if they were just joyful to be free of their isolation on the planet below. If he was in their shoes, the shuttle interior would not have filled him with confidence.

"You should ask them something," Leda whispered next to him.

Cal was confused. "Why? What should I ask them?"

Leda shrugged. "You won't get another chance, I think. Once we get aboard *Fidelity*, contact with these two offworlders will probably become restricted for crew of our rank."

Cal turned and looked at the two imposing, black-clothed figures. He felt suddenly nervous, and his mind blanked.

"You say something to them, then," Cal whispered back to Leda. "It's your only chance too."

The shuttle continued to shake and rumble as it traveled up through the storm.

"Mr. Yendos!" Leda shouted to be heard over the noise.

Cal was slightly shocked she'd done it.

"Mr. Yendos, I have a question," Leda said.

The immense black hood turned to face her.

"Do you know who built that huge starship hulk in this system?" she asked.

Yendos nodded. "It was built by refugees fleeing from the Ancient First Men."

Cal was filled for a moment with total amazement. "Tell us more about them."

Yendos hesitated for a moment. "They caused a terrible genocide."

"Are they still around?" Cal asked. "Are they anywhere near here?"

"A few of their servants remain, buried away, very far from here," Yendos said. "I have encountered a live specimen once."

"Enough questions!" Councilor Theeran called out from the front of the shuttle. "Do not harass our guests."

*

Back aboard the bridge of *Fidelity,* Councilor Theeran and Captain Haran stood behind Cal at his desk, leaning over his shoulder and watching carefully. As Leda had predicted, the offworlders had been taken away to the infirmary as soon as they'd boarded the ship. Reports on his datapad indicated the collection of fuel from the atmosphere had also concluded. Cal was too excited to focus on that. He plugged the black device Yendos had given them into his console. A long series of adapters and converters were required to make the connection.

"Okay, here we go," Cal said as Councilor Theeran and Captain Haran hovered impatiently. "The navigation system is updating now." Everything on his screen changed. "Oh, that's amazing."

Each transit point they'd identified showed new potential routes. Cal leaned in closer. He murmured to himself then became quiet, only his lips moving.

"Well, Operator Heit? Report," Captain Haran ordered tersely.

Cal felt like he was peering into the secret passageways of the universe. All his ideas were being confirmed while, at the same time, he saw how wrong he'd been. Instantly, he received years of improvements to the projects that had defined his life. Yet Cal saw that even Yendos's work was incomplete, showing just the jumps that had been discovered so far. Possibilities continued to radiate out into undefined space. He wished Eevey was there to experience the moment with him.

"Heit?" Haran snapped her fingers at him.

"Can it save us time? Will it get us to the Ruarken Senate faster?" Councilor Theeran asked.

"Absolutely," Cal said. "It does far more than that. I can use these equations to recalibrate all our future journeys. We don't even know how many extra shortcuts this could open up to us."

Theeran stepped away from the console, breathing a sigh of relief, Cal saw.

Captain Haran pointed at one of the jump routes on his screen. "Prepare to bring us to transit out on this route. The pilot will handle getting the ship up to the approach vector." She walked away.

The ship shuddered as it rose through the turbulent, storm-wracked atmosphere, making its way toward the blackness of space.

"Captain! We're detecting another ship in the system. We're visible now we've left the Allumia Eight atmosphere," an operations desk officer reported suddenly.

The bridge crew were immediately all on high alert.

An alarm sounded, not piercingly loud but persistent and anxious. Major Rosco hurried onto the bridge, still wearing his equipment from the planet below.

"On screen," Captain Haran said.

The main screen showed a single large image of a vessel, with labels of scrolling data around it. The resolution their sensors could achieve was not ideal from such a distance, so most surface detail was missing, but the profile of the ship appeared as a blurred three-dimensional image.

"Identify it!" Haran ordered.

"It's the same Enforcer ship that was scanning us in the previous star system," an officer reported. "It's sending out an automatic broadcast that matches our records for common codes. It's demanding all ships acknowledge their presence and recognize its authority."

"Bring us back down into the atmosphere. Get us below the cloud cover!" Executive Theeran said.

The ship dipped below the cloud level again. The rolling waves of vapor washed over their hull once more, and they disappeared into Allumia's turbulence. The dark, alien mass of its inner gas layers swirled beneath them, brooding and simmering.

"Did they detect us?" Theeran asked Captain Haran.

Haran shook her head. "We can't be sure." She addressed the crew. "Shut down all external systems. Bring the engine to the lowest power mode. It's everyone's responsibility to keep this ship hidden at all costs." Captain Haran turned to address Theeran. "We weren't exposed for long, but if the automated message reached us, then it's possible they could have registered our presence. Do you know of any particular reason for them to be following us?"

Theeran smiled in a grim and humorless fashion. "Unfortunately, Captain, we cannot fully guarantee the secrecy of our operation," he said. "Be warned—even on Vale Reach, I suspected the presence of off-world agents amongst us, hidden and reporting as spies. These Enforcers should know nothing of what we do"—Theeran stared at the screen—"but you can never predict failures of judgement."

*

Cal stood in the ship's cafeteria, looking at the messages on the display screen. Their vessel was still hiding from the Enforcer ship in the system. It was a stressful feeling, as all of their mission had been so far, but better than risking a confrontation. He studied the information on the screen, his tray of food still in his hands. What he was reading had brought him to a halt.

"Preserve our free society," the screen said. The words were large and bright.

Cal stared at it, slightly fixated. Then he realized he'd become stationary in the middle of the narrow cafeteria and a small crowd of frustrated people was forming behind him. Cal quickly put his food tray down on a table and took a seat to get out of the way. The screen was still in front of him, with its message. He shook his head and tried to forget about it, but it was on his mind. He took a bite of his food as he continued to stare at it.

Leda took a seat next to him.

"Are we a free society, though?" Cal asked Leda suddenly as he turned, annoyed.

"What?" Leda asked. "What are you talking about?"

"The message on the screen there," Cal said. "The one talking about our free society."

"That was part of the captain's daily general ship briefing today." Leda began to eat her own food.

They usually ate vegetables and stew defrosted from the supplies they'd brought from Vale Reach.

"They've got some guts, posting a message like that," he said.

"How so?" Leda asked.

"Are we a free society?" he loudly asked again.

A few people at neighboring tables turned to look at him briefly.

"No one put a gun to your head and demanded you join this mission," she said.

"That's true," Cal acknowledged, "but there's a gun being held to all of the planet, and they've chosen not to tell anyone. They control the flow of information. They determine exactly what we know, based on what they judge to be appropriate. Is that freedom? We have no idea the ways we're being manipulated."

Leda laughed slightly. "They? Who's they?"

"The government, of course."

"Do you realize how paranoid you sound?"

"Yeah, I know that. But it's a confirmed fact that they know far more than they're letting on. Take this Theeran guy." Cal's voice became quiet and conspiratorial. "What do we know about him? He worked in the intelligence services. Oh, nothing shady there, I'm sure. He tells us this mission has the full backing of the Vale Reach government, but no one else has heard of it, of course. We have only his word that he has the backing. And where did they get the materials to build the reactor? Totally unanswered. They tell us that this ship is under the command of the people of Vale Reach, but there is literally a random offworlder at Theeran's side, directing our decisions. And do not get me started on why we are not allowed to interact with the pilot. I wonder what it is that he knows." Cal waved around a piece of bread as he talked, oblivious to the crumbs.

"Speaking of which," Leda said quietly. "Major Rosco!"

She waved across the cafeteria, and Cal saw Rosco on the other side. Leda waved again, and he came over to where they were sitting.

"Operator Heit and Engineer Palchek, good to see you again," he said. "Are you properly recuperated after our mission down to the planet?"

"I'm getting there," Cal said. "Honestly, I'm not sleeping great. I'm thinking about starting meditation."

"Major Rosco, I have a question," Leda said. "How long are Yendos and Ontu going to be in quarantine for? And when can we speak to them once they're released?"

Rosco shook his head. "That's classified information. I can't give that out."

"What did Theeran offer them in exchange for their transit data?" she asked.

"Theeran didn't offer them anything in exchange," Rosco said.

Leda leaned back and nodded in approval. "Nice."

Rosco sighed in frustration and walked away briskly. "Goddammit," he muttered.

"That was classified, wasn't it?" Cal quietly asked Leda.

*

Fidelity rose out through the storm clouds of Allumia Eight again. They could afford to wait no longer. They'd extracted all the raw materials for fuel they could. Any time lost jeopardized their entire mission to reach Ruarken before their home world was colonized. As they emerged from the atmosphere into empty space, they scanned every corner of the system they could see. No other vessels were there, beyond the long dead hulk—no sign of the Enforcer ship. It had apparently left the Allumia system to continue its patrol elsewhere. *Fidelity* retracted its atmospheric protective panels, made its way to the transit point undetected by anything on the sensors, and left the system.

Chapter 7

Fidelity appeared in the Paxis system. They were cleared to access the star system as a Palladian freighter and could openly announce their presence. Paxis was crowded. Many of the planets were inhabited, but Paxis Prime dwarfed all the others. It was the first major metropolis *Fidelity* had reached, and their research suggested that they had acquired their Palladian visa so easily due to Paxis Prime's lax attitude toward crime and corruption. At least thirty thousand ships filled the space. They would have plenty of crowd to disappear into.

Fidelity would load up on rare fuel rods for the reactor at the markets of Paxis Prime, which offered materials at vastly cheaper rates than Vale Reach had been able to obtain them for. Even the highly unusual heavy metal isotopes the reactor required were available at a location of this size. With the main reactor well supplied, along with the chemicals collected from Allumia, their ship would be fully prepared to tackle whatever awaited them beyond the Grand Highway of Thelmia.

Fidelity broadcast its arrival codes to the Paxis system and received an acceptance signal. The bridge crew breathed a sigh of relief. Similar codes were sent to an orbital station above Paxis Prime, requesting space in a particular berth on the structure. *Fidelity*'s bridge received clearance to dock. That was the first time any of them had seen such a signal, and the bridge crew paused for a moment of satisfaction to admire the welcome message on the main screen as they traveled toward the Paxis Prime orbitals.

The planet's face was in the shadow of its night as they approached, Cal saw, and covered in a sweeping carpet of glimmering lights. He counted at least two dozen elevator tethers that extended up from the world's surface and connected to a network of hundreds of orbital platforms. Each platform was made of gleaming metal. Their arrangement was chaotic, with metal cables threaded between many structures, organically grown over time and too complex and tangled to easily make sense of. The images of the orbital platforms sharpened as they came nearer. Some were covered in mold and lichen that seemed to be reaching for the light. Others seemed to be coated in some form of thick oil-like fluid, perhaps to protect from solar radiation.

As *Fidelity* moved deeper inside the tangled nest of space stations, they were surrounded by starships entering and leaving in every direction. Cal had no duties during the current phase of careful maneuvering, so he waited as *Fidelity* sighted its destination ahead. This station was indistinguishable from the others, but had ten other starships attached to its flank already. Captain Haran quietly issued orders into her personal communicator, presumably to the pilot himself as they came into the dock. A sense of tension grew among the bridge crew, as they had no way to assist in the process.

Cal watched in fascination as the pilot, hidden away in his compartment at the front of the ship, rotated the ship end over end and used the main thruster to decelerate the vessel till they gradually slid into position, facing the slowly spinning orbital station. They approached an empty space on the round surface of the cylindrical station. He admired how elegant the pilot made it look, flawless even. He looked through a series of cameras that showed an exterior view of *Fidelity*.

A flexible tube extended from the orbital station and connected to a hatch on the front of the ship. This was a complex moment in the procedure. Both *Fidelity* and the station maintained artificial gravity through rotation. Combining the two objects whilst maintaining internal gravity was possible, but the number of ways it could be done was very limited. Cal began to understand why the pilot had to be an offworlder, someone with knowledge and familiarity of the unspoken rules of space. Cal was equal parts nervous and thrilled to study the docking maneuver firsthand. That tube would be their access conduit for boarding or leaving the station, as well as a tether that kept them physically attached to its structure. In order to allow *Fidelity* to maintain its consistent artificial gravity, the conduit had connected to a rotating socket port so that their ship would spin even while connected to the side of the immense cylindrical station. *Fidelity* would essentially experience two forms of artificial gravity as it revolved around the center of the orbital station and also around its own central axis. The station reported a comfortable level of gravity in their official broadcasts, low but noticeable. As the metal tube connected fully, all aboard the ship felt a light pull toward the rear of their vessel as *Fidelity* synchronized with the subtle gravity of the station that ran perpendicular to their own. Not much of the equipment on the bridge seemed to shift in any way. The rubberized floors of the ship held the furniture in place effectively. Cal wondered how the canteen was faring, and his own cabin, for that matter.

*

Along with Cal and Leda, Rosco stood at the exit hatch at the front of the ship, waiting for the airlock to open, along with twenty more of *Fidelity*'s crew. Yendos was with them, still in his black suit, having briefly emerged from his medical rest. They were the first batch to go aboard the station though more would soon follow. Visits to places like Paxis Prime would be the only way for the crew of *Fidelity* to leave the inside of the ship. Experiencing time outside was important to maintain their health, and the station at Paxis was as safe an environment as they would get. Rosco had been tasked with supervising the crew as they explored the other side. Meanwhile, another group led by Advocate Fargas would secure the isotope rods at a decent price from a merchant.

They heard the internal movement of the door mechanism. The door rotated away into the frame, revealing a grimy cylindrical corridor made of hinged metal segments. Most of the interior was black from dirt and oxidation. Steel railings led away up all sides of the pipe. A gust of wind rushed down the corridor and pushed them backward. Rosco spat out a mouth full of dust. The press of air reduced after a moment, so they no longer needed to cover their faces with their hands.

"What the hell?" Cal muttered.

The crew looked at each other in uncertainty for a moment. The metal tunnel rattled slightly as it shifted. At the far end of the tunnel, a hatch opened. Beyond was a wide empty space, through which movement was visible. The view of the far side rotated as *Fidelity* and the tunnel continued to roll around the ships central axis. Yendos stepped forward from the group as the others rapidly moved out of his way. He reached up toward the front of his large black hood and adjusted something. A series of small vents and dials was on the surface, Rosco realized.

Yendos sniffed loudly for a moment. "This place will be fine for you all." He sounded weary. Then he turned around and slowly made his way back inside *Fidelity*. Apparently, he had no desire to step aboard the station. The large man disappeared around a corridor.

Rosco turned to address the assembled crew. "You heard him."

He stepped out of the ship and walked along the bottom of the pipe toward the opening at the other end. The rest of the group followed him. The station's gravity pulled them back slightly, and soon they were using handrails to pull themselves forward. At the end, Rosco prepared to cross through the spinning exit hatch, which now felt as though it was above him. The gravity was light, and he pulled himself through easily. One by one, the others came through behind him, entering an enormous open space.

The space station around them was expansive and filled with a huge scaffolding structure. Shop fronts and stalls were positioned on multiple levels, with ladders up and down. Hundreds of people occupied the streets here. The whole area was bustling with activity. In the distance, the curved floor sloped up and out of sight. Several people from the station were close by, sitting on crates and watching them, looking bored. They were a mix of genders and wore similar greasy overalls, with oil patches on their faces. Several smoked pipes. They studied the crew of *Fidelity* with idle disinterest. Their outfits suggested they were workers, and from their attitude, Rosco suspected they were long-term inhabitants of the space station. They seemed to be in no hurry to inspect who was arriving. The lax security seemed strange to Rosco. However, the station had no distinguishing features that set it apart. It was one among very many, and its anonymity was its protection. It was a target to no one. Rosco was envious of them, he realized. That approach used to work for Vale Reach, but no longer. It suddenly struck him as ironic that the depths of a city could provide so much less trouble than a life on the frontier. Rosco waited as more of the *Fidelity* crew continued to climb out of the hatch. One of the lounging station workers nodded to the group and waved for them to move on somewhere. They made no effort to search them in any way.

A hiss sounded to Rosco's right, along with a loud mechanical clang. He turned quickly to see what was happening. Another hatch in the floor was opening thirty meters away. A man exited the hatch, and Rosco realized another starship crew was arriving at the same time they were. Their ship would be the one docked next to *Fidelity*. One by one, other crew members emerged from inside. Rosco was shocked by their appearance. The other newcomers wore some kind of leather bodysuits, stitched together in many places. They were hairless and had tattoos across their bald heads. Many had silver mechanical feet and hands. Rosco tried to stay relaxed and not foolishly gawk at them, but it was hard not to be fixated by their appearance. The newcomers were starting to study the crew of *Fidelity* with similar interest. Rosco turned back to his people. The entire initial party of twenty-four was milling around the arrival point in uncertainty. They looked obviously out of place and somewhere they didn't belong. Rosco gestured for the crew to listen to him, and they huddled close.

"We should spread out to investigate the area. It seems we've arrived in some kind of market. Remember we're supposed to be from a Palladian freighter, so follow your briefings on what to say if anyone questions you. Find out what's in the local vicinity, then meet up back at this spot in thirty minutes."

They nodded and went in different directions through the streets.

*

Rosco walked down an aisle. Shopkeepers were operating their stalls on either side. All the light came from small electric lamps, and visibility was kept low deliberately, it seemed. The low gravity stuck him to the floor loosely, and he naturally walked almost too quickly, having to consciously slow himself down.

Each small shack was cluttered with personal possessions. Children were living in the market. Many of the stores and workshops in the area were operated by families, it seemed. The station wasn't just an orbital platform but a settlement that had been occupied maybe for generations.

The population of Paxis below was massive, Rosco knew. He had trouble imagining how many more people could be amongst the orbital structures.

Rosco suddenly smelled roasted meat. Nothing on *Fidelity* was like it. He arrived at a wide-open area with seating and booths selling food. He saw Cal sitting at a table and decided to check in with him. Rosco walked through the market and sat next to Cal.

"They must import the meat from the planet surface, don't you think?" Rosco asked.

"They must, unless they keep the animals up here," Cal said.

Rosco looked around at the cavernous metal space. "You think they have animals up here?"

Cal shook his head. "I doubt it."

"Feeding a big population in space usually involves eating algae," Leda said. She was wandering around nearby, examining each stall closely. "There has to be some kind of photo-nutrient farm in all these places, ideally connected to the main reactor," she said. "Depending on the efficiency and what kind of growth medium they're using, it might create a carbon cycle where they need nothing more than a little of the reactor's power to keep their inhabitants alive."

"They're eating algae?" Rosco asked. "Is that what we're going to have to eat once the *Fidelity* food supplies run out? That could sap morale."

"There's one way to find out, Major Rosco," Cal pointed at a stall where several sizzling grills cooked a range of skewers. "Go test some. Think of it as part of your duty to *Fidelity*."

Rosco said nothing. Cal could have a valid point. Rosco wondered if he was obligated to try some as part of his reconnaissance of the area. He felt a little queasy at the prospect.

"We'll go with you. You won't be alone for it." Cal got up, ready to walk.

"Do it, Major. We believe in you." Leda was trying not to laugh.

"All right, all right." Rosco got to his feet.

The three of them walked directly toward the food stall.

On the smoking grills was a collection of large insects and rodents. The attendant at the grill, an old woman dressed in the same greasy overalls as everyone else working on the station, flipped the skewers in the fire and applied a thick coat of seasoning to both sides. Leda leaned in close to the heat, fascinated.

"Interested?" Cal asked her.

"Maybe," she said, her mouth open in amazement.

"Here," Rosco said. He took out a small piece of currency ore from his pocket and passed it to Leda. They'd been produced on Vale Reach to a standard they hoped would be universally accepted.

After a few moments, the old woman with the gray hair selected a large insect from the fire, removed it from the skewer to a plastic plate, and pushed it toward Leda. Leda blinked in surprise and gave the old woman the currency ore. She accepted it without a second glance. Leda took the plate, and the three of them walked over to a table.

"Are you going to eat that?" Rosco asked.

"I better had. I don't want to offend them." Leda looked around. "This place is amazing in its own way."

"What did you see when you investigated the area?" Rosco asked them both.

Cal looked around. "Well, I noticed there's—"

Leda took a big bite out of the insect's body.

"God damn," Cal said, staring at her. "Anyway. There's certainly some strange stuff. I've seen plenty of what looks like recharging stations. I think some of the travelers we see here have personal power cells inside their bodies. Their ships can provide electrical energy for them, but any other kind of fuel elements that their ship can't supply will have to come from somewhere like here. Components will burn out and need to be replaced all the time. I've built enough machines to know how they consume resources as they operate. The weirdest part is seeing people actually inserting energy cells directly into their bodies. Look at all the ports on people's stomachs or necks we can see."

"That is very interesting," Leda said. "But I think I've seen something better."

"Better than your giant bug?" Cal asked.

"I saw a guy getting cybernetics installed."

"What, like on the street?"

"Pretty much."

"And when you say installed…?" Rosco asked.

"They really just shoved it into his stump," she replied.

"They did what, now?" Rosco asked. "Was he anesthetized?"

"I guess so," Leda said. "He'd already been injured somehow. He was lying under a sheet, moaning. He looked pretty broken up."

"What happened to him?" Cal asked.

"Could be anything. Maybe he got crushed by something. I've seen plenty of heavy machinery around here," Leda said.

"And when they installed the cybernetics, you're telling me they just pushed the stuff into him?" Cal had turned very pale suddenly.

"Seemed like it was ready to go right away. I could see it moving around seconds after they inserted it," Leda told him.

"Impressive," Rosco said. "Very impressive." He sat back and regarded the other two. "What else?"

Leda and Cal both thought for a second.

"Transport to the planet surface has got to be a big part of what's up here," Cal said. "They have some kind of monorail train that takes people out of this station toward the nearest space elevator, leading to Paxis Prime's surface below. I didn't get a clear look, but the train is probably big enough to carry some heavy equipment."

"That's useful," Rosco said.

"This station is one of the smaller kinds, but I bet they could get anything delivered from the planet below, using the elevators and monorails."

"Interesting to know. Any observations about the structure of this station? Any engineering ideas we could use to improve the ship?"

Cal stared at the ceiling. "It's a wide ring. It looks like it's been built out of modular pieces that have been clamped together. There's multiple layers to the hull. But none of that's very insightful. I guess what's impressive is the way there seems to be this layer of thick grease holding everything together."

"They have one thing here we definitely don't," Leda said. "Interstellar communications lines. There are booths selling bandwidth for FTL messages. Seems in high demand."

"Could we use it to call Vale Reach?" Cal asked quickly, seeming suddenly alert and focused. "We can check in with everyone, make sure things are still okay."

Rosco shook his head. "Accessing the FTL communication lines here is way outside our budget. It's already been considered. These lines are poorly secured. To keep our transmission hidden, we'd have to pay an extreme amount for enough private encryption. It's not worth it. We send our communications when we get to planet Aldethi, not before."

A pressurized hiss sounded behind them. A hatch in the floor opened in the corner of the market, and another crew of men emerged from inside. They all wore the same detailed uniform. The precise ornate features and the strict positioning of their accessories made Rosco instinctively recognize them as military men. Major Rosco's own military uniform, with its badges, seemed plain compared to what they wore. Cal and Leda wore only the regulation work suits of the scientific and engineering departments respectively. Despite the grandeur, the newcomers' outfits seemed somehow worn and faded. They regarded the marketplace with a level of contempt. Their leader turned and scowled at Rosco. He had burn scars across both cheeks and his nose, and both his hands were bionic replacements.

Rosco turned and nodded at the other two. "Let's keep moving."

They got up and walked through several more streets of the marketplace, along ramps and down passageways. Then an abrupt gap appeared between the shops, and they found themselves standing in front of an enormous dome-shaped window looking out to space. They saw the dark, night-covered surface of Paxis Prime below, as well as hundreds of thin strands like spider silk that led between the orbital platforms and the planet. The three of them stopped walking and leaned on the railings to look out for a moment.

"Each kind of light has its own pattern," Leda said. "See, the stars have this ghostly white twinkle. Those sharp orange streaks are the starships moving amongst the platforms. And then you can just about see the dull yellow glow from the settlements where people are living on the planet below."

"It's inspiring," Cal said.

Leda nodded. "I can see nine medium freighters, two heavy freighters—"

"There's no need to count everything," Cal said. "Just absorb the sight in its entirety. Only we get to enjoy the wonder of seeing this." He exhaled in satisfaction. "So where's everyone from on Vale Reach?" he asked.

Neither Rosco nor Leda answered him.

"I'm from a town on the south side," he said. "I was living there with the girl I was going to marry. She's the greatest thing that ever happened to me. She's gorgeous. She's kind. God damn, I was lucky back there." Cal turned to Rosco. "What about you? Anyone you left back home?"

"No, no one," Rosco said. After a second of quiet, he added, "I mean, there's been some girls, obviously."

"I guess army life wouldn't leave much time for women," Cal said.

"I did fine!" Rosco said. "I was very popular! I still am!"

"What about you?" Cal asked Leda.

"I invented half the equipment on the ship. You don't need to know about my personal life," she said.

Rosco smiled. Then his communication device started to ring. He walked a few steps from the others and answered it. Captain Haran was on the line.

"Major Rosco," she said. "We must initiate our first covert operation."

Rosco nodded. "Yes, sir."

"A team is being put together. I'll transfer the briefing now," Haran said. "We'll need someone from science and someone from engineering to be part of this."

Rosco looked over toward where Cal and Leda watched as a massive ship passed the viewing port.

"I know just the two," he said.

*

Leda had never seen inside the bridge's conference room onboard *Fidelity*. She was there with Cal and Rosco, as well as Captain Haran and two other military officers named Major Lee and Major Oryx. The offworlder in the blue suit also sat in the corner, observing everything. The furniture was more luxurious than anything on the rest of the ship, but the room was smaller than she'd expected, with a low ceiling. It was squeezed into a space between the spacious bridge and the exterior hardware decks of *Fidelity*. A ring of white lights in the ceiling was soothing in contrast to the colorful electric displays of the bridge, while a smooth hardwood table filled the center of the room and wood paneling covered the walls. It was genuinely pleasant and calming, almost jarring with the brooding, serious nature of the business that took place there. The table had room for only twelve seats.

"It is time to initiate the next phase of our mission," Captain Haran told them all. "We must upgrade our ship and enhance its abilities to better continue our journey."

The crew all nodded in acknowledgement.

"Our experience with the enhanced checkpoint and the Enforcer ships in the first system has shown us our current signal dampening unit is insufficient for our requirements. Our attempts to emulate a Palladian freighter won't pass any close scrutiny of our electromagnetic emissions," Captain Haran said.

Leda was disappointed but not surprised as she thought about it. The more advanced ships in the galaxy would no doubt have highly sensitive scanning systems. Thinking they could've fooled them all had been optimistic.

"We've located an item, a magnetic dampening unit that can be integrated with the reactor of our ship. This unit will suppress any irregularities in our energy signature that could possibly identify us as not Palladian and allow us to fine-tune how we appear on the scanning systems of other starships. You are to extract it from this location."

She brought up an image of what appeared to be a junkyard onboard the space station they were docked at.

"Science and engineering, your task is to verify that the correct item has been located and to ensure it is extracted properly and ready for use," Captain Haran told Cal and Leda. "Our scouts have already studied the perimeter. Break through the fence here. At the same time, we'll create a significant distraction in the shop front to attract most of their staff."

The image switched to a map of the streets on the space station.

"This region is where the station stores parts that it's harvested from derelict starships while the merchants search for a buyer, though we don't have the funds to make a purchase. They currently have a backlog of parts, and it's minimally guarded, by our analysis." Haran pointed at a specific street. "Progress along this route then break into the junkyard here at this point. Remember, you must verify that it's something usable that we can integrate into our systems. We leave as soon as the dampening unit is fully installed."

Captain Haran wrapped up her briefing, and the other officers prepared to leave the room.

Cal leaned over and whispered to Leda, "Are we stealing this thing?"

"Yes, we are," Leda said. "It's for the survival of our planet."

Cal seemed unconvinced. "This is going to get us into trouble with someone."

"We could ask the legal counsel," Leda whispered, nodding toward the offworlder in the corner.

Leda leaned over to speak to the man without anyone else noticing. "How illegal is this going to be?"

"You're not my client," he replied with a smile. "So I don't have to answer that."

Chapter 8

Cal huddled with Leda behind Rosco and the other two security officers at the edge of a wire fence, fifteen feet high and topped with razors. They'd disembarked from *Fidelity* once more and traveled through the back alleyways of the space station's marketplace. They'd followed the path indicated on the map in the briefing room without difficulty. Now, they were at the rear perimeter fence of the scrap merchant that they'd identified as their target. Major Lee and Major Oryx were keeping watch on both sides of the alley, but their team seemed to be alone in the secluded alleyway. The military officers each carried a pair of handguns, a primary weapon and a reserve. Suddenly, the electrical lights throughout the whole area shut down, plunging them into blackness.

"That's our distraction," Rosco said. "Cut through that fence."

Leda pulled out a gas-powered blowtorch and ignited the flame. It made little sound but released a small blue light. In less than twenty seconds, Leda had cut a hole in the wires big enough for people to crawl through.

Inside the scrapyard, pieces of machinery were piled high in stacks. If they were pieces of starships, then they'd each been sliced up into to something only a few meters in length. Several motorized cranes were nearby, for moving pieces around. The low gravity of the station would make everything easy to lift. With the electrical power out, the blackness made any details hard to see. As they moved forward, the crew tried to stay sheltered and hidden in the narrow crevices between tall mounds of junk.

They didn't have information on where exactly the item they were seeking might be in this region. It was up to Cal and Leda to recognize what they were searching for. Rosco led them along, working their way inward from the hole they'd cut. Leda and Cal rapidly checked the scrap material they passed on either side, hunting for the magnetic dampening unit.

Everyone stayed silent, straining to hear any sound of human contact ahead, each doing everything in their power to tread quietly. Any misstep caused the soft scrape of metal on metal in the terrain of the junkyard. Distant, angry voices were audible from the front of the junkyard, which would hopefully cover any noises they made. Cal looked around at the dark mountains of junk—still no sign of their objective.

Electric lights suddenly popped back into existence, and everyone could see each other clearly. The five of them looked around in anxious shock.

Cal's heart was racing. Then he saw what he needed. "There it is." He pointed toward the top of a nearby stack that loomed over them.

"Yeah, that's what we need," Leda agreed.

"Can you get it down fast?" Rosco asked.

The voices from the front of the scrapyard had fallen silent.

"Maybe," Leda said. "Maybe if the gravity's light enough." Leda jumped surprisingly far, and landed high the junk mound, next to the magnetic dampening unit.

Cal wasn't sure he shared her confidence. Rosco jumped up after her, and the two of them tugged on the metal unit together. It was around four feet in length, and it shifted slightly as they pulled at it. The top of the stack wobbled ominously, threatening to come down on them. Cal jumped up and arrived next to them, his nerves on edge. The three of them tried to work the item free from its place in the junk pile.

"Let me check its ports." Leda released her grip and crouched down low to quickly study the unit's underside.

"Do we have the cables for it on the ship?" Cal asked.

"Looks like they're all standard connections," Leda said with a smile.

When *Fidelity* had been constructed, Vale Reach had been able to reverse engineer a few of the most common types of ports and connections they estimated off-world ships would use.

"Someone's coming," one of the security officers said back on the ground level.

Cal looked around from his vantage point up on the junk mound. A group of people was moving directly toward them through the junkyard. He didn't have time to study them.

Suddenly, the magnetic dampening unit popped free from the stack of machinery, and the three of them slipped and tumbled down to the ground level with the unit. They all landed on their feet after a slow descent.

Cal and Leda picked up the unit between them. It was lighter than expected, but its bulky shape was hard to carry easily.

"Get out of here—go," Rosco said, pushing the two of them along the path back to the fence.

Cal was ready to make a swift exit and needed no encouragement to start moving.

*

Major Rosco drew his pistol, took the safety off, and checked the ammo. Major Lee and Major Oryx did the same.

"Are you ready?" Rosco asked. "Let's not try to kill anyone. If we're lucky, we can just threaten them and create a delay while the others escape."

"Go with them, Rosco," Major Lee said. "Make sure those two get out of here with the unit. Oryx and I will slow down the people here." He waved for Rosco to go.

Rosco saw Lee had a point. Someone had to keep an eye on the others while they escaped.

"Don't do anything too reckless," he said to them.

Major Lee and Oryx nodded.

Rosco turned and hurried down the path Cal and Leda had taken. He caught up with them quickly and squeezed past them to lead the way through the tangled collection of metal. Everything looked different since the bright electric light had returned. Rosco turned a corner and was confronted by four men wearing greasy overalls. Each carried a kind of shotgun and didn't seem surprised to meet them there. Rosco stopped and raised his hands. They were outnumbered and outgunned. It was far too dangerous to raise his own weapon. Cal and Leda came from behind him, still carrying the magnetic dampening unit. They froze when they saw the hostile men but kept hold of the unit. Rosco quickly surveyed the group who'd intercepted them, noting how their clothes and skin were stained with oil from the scrapyard. All four were either old or very weathered. The man at the front gestured for Rosco, Cal, and Leda to face away and line up against a nearby bulkhead. Cal and Leda looked at Rosco, and he nodded for them to comply. They let go of the unit and turned to stand side by side, facing the rusted metal surface of a starship's decaying flank.

A deafening crack sounded, and gunfire tore through the air. Rosco pushed Cal and Leda to the ground and jumped to look back. Major Lee and Major Oryx had appeared at the top of a large tower of scrap. They were firing their pistols at the scrapyard workers, who scrambled away from them in sudden confusion and panic as they sought cover. Rosco grabbed Cal and Leda from the ground and pulled them to their feet again. He shoved them away from the area down another path toward the fence. The two of them grabbed the dampening unit once again and ran down the path. Rosco ran after them, then he stopped and turned back.

Major Lee and Major Oryx were still exchanging fire against the scrap crew, shooting with their pistols while their adversaries fired back with their shotgun-type weapons. The two security officers were at a clear disadvantage. After a flurry of gunfire, Lee and Oryx both made a dash down the junk slopes toward Rosco's position. One of the scrap workers reached inside his overalls and pulled out a tubular device. He tossed it into the path of Lee and Oryx, and Rosco watched in shock, realizing it was a grenade as it bounced along the ground.

A blinding blue flash left his eyes burning painfully, and he heard an angry hiss of chemicals igniting. When his vision returned, Lee and Oryx had turned pitch black. They crumbled into piles of glowing orange embers, leaving only ash where the two men had stood.

"Holy fuck." Rosco turned and ran at full speed after Leda and Cal.

Cal and Leda had reached a junction and were looking around in confusion. The fence wasn't where they'd expected it to be. There was no sign of it at all. They must have taken a wrong turn somewhere amid the narrow paths between the massive engines and starship valves. Rosco chose a route and ran down a path to keep them moving.

"Follow me! Keep up!" he shouted.

He arrived at a wide-open area containing a small shuttlecraft with its interior lights on. It seemed deserted, but he slowed down warily just in case.

"Could this get us out of here?" Rosco asked Cal and Leda.

"It's powered up. It might work," Cal said.

"Do you think it has fuel?" Leda asked.

"Shit, are we going to have to refuel it?" Cal asked as they looked at each other in uncertainty.

Rosco heard the sounds of the angry scrap workers from not far behind them.

"Get this shuttle operational," Rosco told them. "Take it up into the air and get back to *Fidelity* with the dampening unit as soon as you can."

"What are you doing?" asked Leda.

Rosco looked back the way they'd come. Without anyone to slow them down, the scrapyard workers were probably approaching rapidly.

"I'm going to delay the people coming after us until you get the shuttle engines running. Take off as soon as you're able to. I'll join you when I can," Rosco said. Given what'd happened to Lee and Oryx, he wasn't sure if he could manage to slow their assailants down for long at all. He checked both his pistols were fully loaded and took up a defensive position behind a large metal turbine.

*

Cal and Leda dashed toward the shuttle, dragging the magnetic dampening unit behind them. They skidded to a halt as they reached it. They set down the unit as Cal hurriedly examined the shuttle, while Leda checked around the exterior. It seemed unoccupied, as though the operators had suddenly left. He found an open ramp and cautiously went aboard. Leda quickly joined him, and the two of them searched its small interior. The ship had been halfway prepared for launch, but the process was incomplete. Leda picked up a handful of cables and muttered to herself as she studied them. Cal went inside the cockpit. The controls seemed to have power though he couldn't read the symbols on any of them.

"Do you think we can get this thing moving?" he asked, looking over his shoulder at Leda.

She was checking a dial on the wall. "I think the reserve tank still has fuel, but it needs to be connected to the engine. What about Rosco?"

Cal gritted his teeth. He felt terrified, but the weight of guilt was also immense on him. "We can't abandon him here," he said as he tried to think through their options. "We need to get him on to the shuttle somehow."

Leda patted him on the shoulder and pointed toward something on the wall. A large machine gun hung there, designed to be carried by two people, complete with long belts of ammunition.

"Do you think we could?" Cal asked.

Leda took it down from the wall.

*

Rosco shot at the scrap workers immediately as they came into view. He sensed he didn't have the luxury of warning shots. The men were just defending their property, but if they were a threat to the success of his mission, they couldn't be allowed to jeopardize Vale Reach. He had a duty to protect all the crew, especially Cal and Leda. He was the one who'd brought them to this place. Rosco let out a deep exhalation and fired another burst of shots as some of the scrap workers peered out of cover. He still hadn't hit anybody. A single plasma grenade had killed Lee and Oryx, and Rosco had little doubt they'd have more. At any moment, he could be vaporized by the flash heat of a plasma detonation. He couldn't even imagine what other superior weapons they might have ready to use against him.

A bullet struck the ground next to him, seemingly fired from a sniper's position. Another hit the metal pipe he was sheltering behind and ricocheted nearby. He cursed and hunched down lower. Several more sniper shots hit around his position, and he lay flat on the ground to try to stay out of sight. He had no idea where the shooter was.

A sudden loud, roaring torrent of gunfire deafened him momentarily. It ceased briefly, followed by another burst of fire, then another, each a long, continuous stream of bullets. Rosco looked up from his position to see Cal and Leda carrying an unfeasibly large cannon, with a belt of ammunition that stretched back to the shuttle. Leda stood at the front, holding the trigger, while Cal kept the weapon loaded from behind. Rosco scrambled toward them, crawling as fast as he could. He heard gunshots from the scrap workers behind him, but they dared not aim for a clear shot while Cal and Leda had the cannon. Leda periodically sprayed more bullets in their direction.

Rosco covered the last of the open ground and ran past them. "Let's go! I hope you've got it working."

The three of them ran aboard the shuttle. Cal hit a button in the interior, and the entrance ramp slowly rose up and closed.

"You came back for me," Rosco said, trying to recover his breath. "Thank you."

"Neither of us knew how to fly the shuttle," Leda said.

"You didn't need to tell him that," Cal said.

"It's fine—it's fine," Rosco said. "Which way are the controls?"

Cal led him to the cockpit, where Rosco took a seat. He didn't understand any of the button labels, but he recognized enough to get the shuttle moving. Rosco tested the flight stick.

"They're here!" Cal shouted. "The scrap workers have figured out what we're doing."

"Did we lock the access ramp?" Leda asked.

"I didn't know how," Cal said.

"What?" Rosco shouted over his shoulder.

"And I'm pretty sure there's a manual-release lever on the outside that can open it," Cal said.

They had no more time to test the controls.

"Hold on to something. I'm getting us out of here," Rosco said.

Rosco grabbed an appropriate-looking lever and increased what he thought was the throttle. The whole shuttle lifted rapidly up into the air. Rosco hurried to decrease the throttle again, trying to get them level at a steady position before they hit some kind of ceiling. Not much light from the lower areas of the station reached this high, and so it was difficult to ascertain just how much space he actually had. A collision with any kind of machinery could be fatal. Rosco estimated there was about five meters in which to fly the shuttle craft.

"Do you see any heavy weapons among the scrap workers?" Rosco asked urgently. They weren't visible from his cockpit position. He had to rely on the other two looking through the side windows.

"They're talking about something," Cal said. "They seem to be having a debate. I mean, I guess this is their own shuttle. Okay, it seems they've reached a decision. They're about to start shooting at the shuttle. Yes, I can see some big, heavy weapons. Now, go!"

Rosco opened a different throttle, and the shuttle rushed forward.

They were out of the scrapyard, somewhere high above the food stalls of the market. For a moment, Rosco was uncertain what to do next.

"We need to get out into space. This shuttle is sealed for it. The ramp will lock itself when we get into the vacuum," Leda said. "Find an airlock for the shuttle, preferably an automatic airlock."

Rosco cursed. "We've not thought this through. I'm sure the people on the station have some way of following this shuttle. There's likely some kind of tracking device in here."

Leda made a sudden excited noise, which puzzled him. "I have a solution for this! I can connect our magnetic dampening unit to this shuttle right now. We can make this shuttle invisible to any scanning systems."

"Can you?" Cal asked.

From Rosco's seat in the cockpit, he could only hear their voices. Then he heard the dampening unit being dragged across the shuttle interior.

"Help me with this," Leda told Cal.

"Pass me those cables," Cal said.

They were silent for a few minutes. Rosco shut off the shuttle's lights to better hide it. He could see very little of what was around them in the upper heights of the deck. It took concentration to keep them hovering inside the space station. The sounds of items clattering and rattling filled the interior.

"I don't think the shuttle's designed to be used this way," Rosco said.

Despite all his efforts to keep the shuttle stationary, the rotating nature of the space station's interior made the shuttle seem to be constantly falling toward the ground.

"How's it looking?" he asked.

He had no idea how visible they were from the promenade below. Potentially, many people were watching them.

Cal appeared in the cockpit. "Ready."

The magnetic dampening unit emitted a deep hum that almost made Rosco's teeth rattle.

Cal looked out through the main screen next to Rosco. "There!" He pointed toward a wide circular opening in a wall, large enough for the shuttle to enter.

"Are you sure about this?" Rosco asked. "That seems like some kind of tunnel."

Leda joined them in the cockpit. "Get us inside there." She pointed at the open hole.

Rosco directed the shuttle toward the hole. "Okay, I'm taking us in."

He slowly maneuvered the shuttle into what he saw was a wide cylindrical tube. The interior was totally dark, but the shuttle provided a sensor image of their immediate surroundings, showing they were at one end of a long, winding pipe.

"What is this thing for?" Cal muttered.

"Maybe some kind of exhaust vent," Leda said.

Rosco carefully flew the shuttle ahead, using the sensor images to follow the path of the tunnel in the darkness. Its winding length took twenty minutes to navigate, which felt like an eternity. Suddenly, a pair of mechanical doors slammed shut behind them. Then a loud pop sounded as the air pressure changed.

"What's happening?" Rosco asked.

"We've entered a valve," Leda said.

The front end of the pipe ahead of them had a flat surface.

"We've reached the exterior of the hull," Cal said.

Maneuvering through the pipes had completely distorted their sense of up and down. The shuttle floor beneath their feet had become a steep slope without them realizing. They all subconsciously clung on tightly to the side of the shuttle to steady themselves.

"How do we get out of here?" Rosco asked.

"We should be ejected when the station vents its exhaust gases," Cal said.

Rosco rotated the shuttle, and Cal and Leda struggled not to fall over.

A metal door opened in front of them, revealing a mesh covering that led to the open void of space. All sound outside immediately disappeared. Rosco made a judgment call. He hit the accelerator, and their shuttle craft tore through the mesh screen. They were out in space.

*

"*Fidelity*, *Fidelity*, come in," Rosco said over the junkyard shuttle's radio system.

They were floating through the empty vacuum. The shuttle had no gravity onboard since they'd successfully ejected from the station. Rosco had never operated a true voidcraft before, but in some ways, it was simpler than any aircraft. The challenge was not colliding with so many other objects that were drifting in space: abandoned hardware, cables and tethers between the stations, and garbage. The main shipping lanes between the platforms were kept clear of junk, but the three of them had agreed their safest choice was to avoid those highly visible areas. Every few minutes, some heavy object would clunk loudly off the side of their ship. The craft had rockets on all sides, and Rosco used those to nudge them along carefully. The shuttle crawled awkwardly forward in slow search of *Fidelity*.

"How's the dampening unit holding up, Leda?" he asked.

He heard a busy grunt of affirmation from the other room.

"Are we still fully hidden?" he asked.

They were close to some large starships outside the station.

Cal stuck his head around the door to the cockpit. "It's all good. This thing is designed to cloak signals for ships far bigger than this. It should be able keep us invisible from everything except good old-fashioned visible light. Someone did put this unit in a scrap heap, though."

"Please identify yourself," the radio responded.

They'd been transmitting a signal requesting contact with *Fidelity* as they drifted through space.

"*Fidelity*! This is Major Nurten Rosco. I am piloting an unidentified captured shuttle as part of an authorized assignment under the captain. We need to dock with the ship as soon as possible. Please acknowledge."

After a pause on the line of about ten seconds, the person replied, "Acknowledged. You are authorized to approach the *Fidelity* shuttle bay."

"Where the hell are they?" Cal asked.

The three of them still hadn't been able to figure out operating the long-range scanning equipment on the shuttle, so they had no choice but to visually identify each starship docked at the space station. Rosco tried hard to fly smoothly to avoid suspicion, but the shuttle moved erratically under his control as they passed from ship to ship, trying to study the outline of each vessel in the dim illumination emitted from the station. Their own headlamps were kept low to reduce attention.

"There!" Rosco pointed at something through the cockpit window. "That's it, right?"

They recognized the black cigar shape of *Fidelity* against the electric lights of the orbital stations.

Cal celebrated. "Hell, yes. Get us in there."

They watched as *Fidelity*'s rear launch bay doors opened. None of them had ever seen the doors operate from the outside before. The entrance was large enough but constantly rotating away from them under *Fidelity's* spinning motion.

"You can do this, right?" Cal asked. "Get us in and stuck to the landing pad, preferably the right way up."

"No problem," Rosco said.

*

The shuttlecraft landed in the *Fidelity* launch bay with a loud clunk. Rosco shut the engine off a little early, and they dropped the final half meter of distance. Dozens of technicians from the engineering department ran up to the shuttle, carrying fire extinguishers and tools. Rosco hit a button to open all the shuttle's ramps and lay back in his chair, stretching his arms in satisfaction. "My god, it's good to be back." The familiar walls of *Fidelity's* interior, even the smell and taste of the air onboard felt euphoric. "We did it." Then he fell silent as he remembered Major Lee and Major Oryx would never be coming back.

An alarm sounded suddenly, and he looked around in concern. The alarm was coming from inside *Fidelity,* not the shuttlecraft. Lights flashed in the hangar bay, and confusion spread among the engineers. Rosco got up from the pilot's chair, groaning as his muscles ached. All his adrenaline was fading. Cal and Leda were still in the shuttle's cargo bay, surrounded by many more engineers detaching cables from the magnetic dampening unit.

"What does that noise mean?" Rosco asked. He pointed outside the ship, where the alarms blared.

An engineer from the hangar bay passed him a datapad. He read the alert status. The Enforcers' ship had been sighted again in the current star system and was approaching Paxis Prime. Potentially, the Enforcers' ship could have already sighted *Fidelity*. It was certainly heading right toward their position.

Rosco swore again and paced up and down for a second.

Leda pulled out the last of the cables. "Get this thing to the engine room." She waved for the other engineers to take it out. The hangar bay engineers picked up the machine and hurried down the shuttle ramp with it.

Cal and Leda slumped to the floor in exhaustion. For a moment, all three of them were silent inside the shuttle.

Leda looked at Cal and Rosco. "We should probably make sure they install it properly."

Cal sighed in frustration. "You're right."

They got to their feet, and all three ran wearily down the shuttle ramp. They passed through the corridors of *Fidelity* to the engine room. Like the bridge, it was a cylindrical room in the core of the vessel, with an axis of zero gravity at its center. That central axis was fully occupied by the main segment of *Fidelity's* reactor, a huge object that was covered in thick, protective metal plating and occasionally releasing an ominous blue flash. The room around the reactor was filled with computer terminals.

"Let's clamp it on directly," an engineer said.

Rosco waited at the doorway, watching what was happening, whilst Cal and Leda moved past him and checked the computer screens. The reactor was at least three meters above all their heads. Leda hit a button, and a large section of the room rose under their feet, lifting them up.

Cal quickly stepped off the platform and joined Rosco at the doorway. "I hate getting close to that thing," he told Rosco.

Leda and the other engineers came within arm's reach of the immense reactor.

"What can we do to help them?" Rosco asked.

"Oh, you? You're kind of useless here," Cal told him. He looked up at the machine. "I mean, at least I understand what they're doing. I just don't plan on being the one to actually do it." He patted his uniform. "I'm science department. We keep it theoretical."

The engineers together rotated the magnetic dampening unit onto its back and lifted it up above their heads. It occurred to Rosco how much easier the action was in the lower-gravity environment of the room's center. Under stress, the engineers moved as an effective team, as though they shared one mind. The dampening unit made contact with the round surface of the giant reactor's metal shield and seemed to immediately stick itself in place.

Rosco breathed a sigh of relief. "Is that it? Is it done?"

"No, it still needs to charge up before it does anything," said Cal.

Rosco tried not to let his frustration show. He checked his datapad and saw the Enforcer ship was closing in quickly. *Fidelity* had just under a minute until they were potentially in weapons range. If the Enforcer ship got near enough to establish a visual lock, *Fidelity* would have difficulty escaping, even with the dampening unit. They had to get away from their current position while they still had a chance.

The whole ship shook with a rumble. The reactor above them released a brief, strobing flicker that hurt Rosco's eyes. Captain Haran had given the order for them to break free from their berth on the space station. He checked the datapad. All their crew had already withdrawn safely from the space station.

The docking tube from *Fidelity* to the station was detached. The ship rattled all over for a moment as it rapidly accelerated away from the docking ring. The nuclear thruster engaged to full power, and the reactor flared with angry blue light above them. *Fidelity* sped away from the station, but the Enforcer ship was still gaining on them, according to the datapad.

"Leda?" Rosco shouted up at her. "We need the unit to work right now!"

A moment of silence passed, beneath the electrical crackle of the reactor's core.

"It's done!" she yelled back.

He looked at his datapad. The Enforcer ship continued on its path toward the space station, but its journey would no longer intercept theirs. *Fidelity* adjusted its own direction, and the Enforcer ship still didn't change its path. It began to reduce its acceleration. They'd evaded its sensors.

Rosco exhaled and sat down on the floor. His hands were shaking.

Cal patted him on the back. "Now, I think we did it."

His communication line came back online. "Major Rosco, Councilor Theeran and Captain Haran want to see you in the conference room," someone said.

*

The captain and the councilor were waiting for Rosco when he arrived on the bridge, plus the lawyer, Fargas, who seemed to skulk perpetually in the background.

"Major, thank you for joining us," Captain Haran said slowly. Like many high-ranking officers he'd met, she became dangerously quiet when angry. "Report to us on your actions."

Rosco knew exhaustion was no excuse to compromise on a debriefing. He started with the positive aspects. "We've completed our operation to obtain a magnetic dampening unit and successfully installed the unit to enhance the stealth capabilities of the ship." Rosco paused for a second. "As I understand it, we've been able to lose the vessel pursuing us."

"Barely in time," Councilor Theeran said. "They've been confused by the change of our energy signature. However, plenty of other ships just observed us conduct an unscheduled emergency detachment from that station, followed by a high-power thruster burn to keep us out of an Enforcer ship's close detection range. Then our signal literally vanished in empty space. We have not reduced whatever suspicion our vessel is under, and this is certainly not typical behavior for the Palladian freighter we claim to be. To what degree do you honestly think we got away with that?"

Rosco didn't know how to respond.

Theeran sighed deeply in frustration and indicated he was done talking.

"Where are Major Lee and Major Oryx?" Captain Haran asked.

"They were killed by hostiles in a gunfight at the scrapyard." Rosco hesitated. "They fought bravely. We owe our success to them."

Advocate Fargas reached over and patted Councilor Theeran on the arm. "I think it's best if you don't know the specifics of this event."

Theeran looked Major Rosco up and down and shook his head in sadness. "Our first two officers lost," he said. "They've given us everything. We'll owe them a debt forever. We need to redouble our efforts to make sure nothing about this mission is in vain."

Fargas and Theeran walked away and left the conference room.

"Take a rest, Major," Captain Haran said. "We'll take up a safe position close to the next transit point and conduct a full diagnostic test on the ship's systems before we leave. Be ready by then."

*

Cal sat in the *Fidelity* canteen, staring ahead in an unfocused way. He held a breadstick in his hand but hadn't taken a bite in some time. An image was on the wall in front of him, a landscape containing a single enormous green mountain. All around it was a ring of smaller gray rocky peaks, and above was a sky filled with streaks of white and gold.

Major Rosco walked past his table.

"I've been to those mountains, you know," Cal said, pointing at the picture. "I've stood right where that image was taken."

Rosco stopped and looked at the image. "I was actually stationed in the mountains there for several years."

Cal turned and looked up at him. "That potentially explains a lot about you." He turned back to the picture. "They're filled with Sirkallion tunnels underneath, you know?"

"Of course I know," Rosco said. "I led some of the reconnaissance teams that were mapping out the uncharted regions in the tunnels."

They heard another voice. "Do you think it's true that the Sirkallions built them all?" Leda came over and joined them at Cal's table.

Rosco almost laughed at the way she seemed to appear from nowhere. "Why don't I tell you about it?" he said and sat in a nearby chair. "The Sirkallions didn't build those tunnels at all. The tunnels definitely predate them. We did find some derelict Sirkallion equipment in there, but they were exploring those tunnels just as we were."

"Wow." Leda rubbed her hands together as she considered the idea. "Amazing."

"There's remnants of Sirkallion structures all over Vale Reach," Cal said. "They removed everything valuable, but they left plenty of junk. I heard theories that the remaining structures are all somehow linked to the tunnels, like the Sirkallions were searching for something in there," Cal said.

"Could be," Rosco replied. He thought about it. "How would that work?"

Cal began to sketch shapes on the table using his finger. "You see, the structures are scanning stations. They're spread around the planet to try to measure what's under the earth. Then the Sirkallions would enter into the blocked tunnels to try and reach a specific point."

"Is there really evidence for that?" Leda sounded very uncertain.

"No one knows how deep the tunnels are," Rosco said. "They're eerie when you get down there. It's like they branch off in more directions the deeper down you go. The limiting factor for us was keeping a supply chain able to move in fresh oxygen and removing the rubble from unexplored areas."

"So the tunnels under Vale Reach are definitely man-made?" Leda asked.

Rosco nodded. "I think so."

Leda smacked her hand on the table. "There's so much about our own planet we don't know. We've found relics from all kinds of civilizations, but none of their wisdom made it through. When I think of how little we know about ourselves, it drives me crazy. How do we live like this?"

Rosco shrugged. "I honestly never found the time to study ancient history."

"How can we face whatever's out there in space when we don't even know our own past? How can we understand our place in things if we don't see the limits of our current experience?" Leda asked. "Vale Reach is backward. There, I said it!"

A few seconds of silence passed.

"Wow, Leda. Wow," Cal said. "I can't believe you insulted the entire planet." Then he laughed.

Rosco sighed and looked unhappy.

"And at a time like this? Attacking Vale Reach while it's down?" Cal said. "Hasn't our world suffered enough without your scathing commentary as well?" He snorted as he laughed uncontrollably. "Those poor bastards, they have no idea…"

"Is he having some kind of breakdown?" Rosco said jokingly as Cal continued to howl with laughter.

"Who knows?" Leda said. "He might always be like this." She turned to Rosco. "I'm sorry I insulted our planet. I know you've been working very hard to protect it. I can see Vale Reach means a lot to you."

Rosco laughed out loud. "Don't worry about it."

Chapter 9

Alarms went off in Cal's cabin, and he sat up in abrupt shock. It felt like only minutes had passed since he'd reached his bed. Several warnings were blaring, he realized. His communications device was flashing angrily. Cal was required on the bridge, top priority. He picked up his uniform from the floor and hurriedly dressed again. He dashed through the corridors of the ship and stumbled onto the bridge. Immediately, he saw everyone's faces were grave. The officers were totally focused on their consoles. Captain Haran looked up and glared at Cal. His heart rate raced as he saw the bridge's main screens.

"We jumped to a new system," he said.

"We've jumped incorrectly, Operator Heit," the captain told him. "We are not at all where we're supposed to be. Figure it out now."

Cal ran to his desk and looked at an analysis on his console. They'd jumped successfully through the transit point, using the launch vector he'd programmed into the system a few hours previous. Yet they were definitely not where they expected to be. The environment here didn't seem to be on any of their star maps.

More staff were rushing onto the bridge, including Rosco and Leda. A red alert had been sounded across the whole ship.

"Go through every piece of data, every scrap of archive material that we have. We need to identify where we are immediately," Captain Haran said. "Get Yendos in here from wherever the hell he is."

To return the way they'd come would incur a massive time debt, Cal saw. Performing a U-turn would put maximum strain on the FTL drive unless they allowed a cool-down time.

"I'm picking up starship signals," Leda said. "Lots of them, too many to count, easily more than thousands. They're coming from nearly every planet in the system and the moons too—at least a hundred different cluster locations."

"Is the dampening unit still active?" Captain Haran asked.

"Yes, sir."

"Take us quickly to open space, below the orbital plane," Captain Haran ordered. In the empty regions far from the planets, they were less likely to be observed. Haran pointed at the main screen. "Show me what we're looking at."

Images of planets surrounded by orbital structures appeared across the screen like a cloud of particles. A triple binary solar structure created a dazzlingly complicated arrangement of planets and asteroid clusters scattered around them. Some of the largest settlements were around the upper regions of gas giants among an ecosystem of thousands of lunar objects. The number of space-bound colonies far exceeded the number of terrestrial ones. Cal realized he couldn't see any terrestrial colonies at all.

"There's a message from the pilot's cockpit," one officer said. "He says he's figured out where we are."

"Put it to my private channel," Captain Haran said. She listened intently to what he said for a few moments. "Transfer the information up on screen."

Thousands of labels appeared, connected to all the data points.

"Oh shit," Cal said under his breath. These ships on the screen became registered as pirate vessels, marauders, and raiders—each one of them.

Captain Haran pointed at Cal. "You. Into the conference room. Now."

*

Cal sat in the conference room. Captain Haran came to join him, as did Councilor Theeran and Advocate Fargas.

"Did you enter the equations correctly?" Haran immediately asked him.

"Yes," Cal replied. He couldn't understand what had gone wrong. "I double-checked. Everything was entered into the computer exactly as we planned. There was no error inputting the commands." He hesitated for a moment. "Where are we?" he asked.

Fargas spoke up. "This system is supposedly the territory of an alliance called the Black Squid Organization," Advocate Fargas said. "They don't have diplomatic relations with any civilized societies. Pirates like these are generally considered to be universally hostile."

"I think we can say this is not 'supposedly' their territory," Haran said. "We're completely surrounded by them. It appears we've avoided their attention so far, but it's unknown if we'll remain undetected for the duration of our journey here." She turned to focus on Cal. "Do you understand how seriously this has jeopardized everything?"

Cal held up his hands. His heart was beating so quickly that he was struggling to think. "I don't understand. I cross-referenced everything using theories that we all agreed to accept as valid. If our foundational principles are wrong, then we don't know anything at all."

Captain Haran stared coldly at him. He sensed he'd not given her the right answer.

Cal attempted to clarify. "This jump was calculated using the additional harmonics patterns that were shown to us by the offworlder we picked up. The integration parameters we used here were derived from his data."

Haran turned to Councilor Theeran for an explanation.

"Cartographer Yendos has chosen to remain in his cabin for most of the journey so far, suffering from allergies, he reports, from his exposure to our ship's atmosphere," Theeran said. "I think it's time we bring him up here to review things with us."

Captain Haran nodded and issued a command into her comms channel for Yendos to be brought to join them.

Cal experienced a growing concern that he had only increased the trouble he faced.

Haran, Theeran, and Fargas continued to discuss their options. Cal was not part of that conversation. He sat waiting for what felt like long minutes until Yendos arrived. Cal was amazed once again by the man's long black coat and how unnaturally broad he seemed. As ever, the coat's hood was completed sealed, hiding Yendos's face, and his hands were wrapped in black gloves.

He took a seat at the conference table and seemed to regard Cal in a displeased manner, his feet spread wide and his head titled. He could communicate an amazing amount of body language through the thick body suit covering his chest and head. His outfit looked to be made of leather, but Cal doubted it had come from a living animal. Despite its thick, all-enclosing material, Yendos seemed perfectly comfortable in it.

"I hear this is the ensign that has questioned my work," Yendos told Theeran, disdain in his voice.

Cal decided to stand by his own work. "I'm actually a technical science officer. I applied the principles you gave us, exactly as described in your notes. You showed us the existence of these extra transit routes. If the routes are as you described, then the approach vector should have translated us to our target system perfectly. I can demonstrate, with calculations, how the transit route that brought us here cannot be exactly as you've described. Nothing else explains our situation. The only way we could get launched at an unpredictable angle is if we hit the transit point with a faulty alignment."

Yendos leaned back in surprise as though fully incredulous. "I pioneered those routes myself. They are a vital part of my great achievements in mapping the galaxy. Obviously, you have failed to apply my work properly."

Cal felt a sense of wonder for a moment. "Did you really discover these routes yourself? They're outside of any conventional star maps we've ever seen. I think they're commonly assumed to not be real, something close to legendary." Yendos's mind must contain vast knowledge, Cal thought, answers to mysteries they'd never even conceived of.

"Do not place undue emphasis on the opinions of the common man," Yendos said. "The truth is rarely as convenient as people expect it to be."

Cal was enthralled by the prospect of Yendos's secrets. "I don't even know what happens if someone attempts an experimental transit and gets it wrong," he said. "They might end up stranded anywhere."

"Operator Heit, I think we are experiencing exactly what can happen in that event," Captain Haran interjected. "What I need is for you to explain exactly how it went wrong."

Cal nodded and turned back to Yendos. "This knowledge—"

Yendos interrupted him. "Is not shared lightly! There is more value in knowledge than anything else. Do not lose sight of the gifts I have given you. Even the confirmed existence of these routes is a precious secret."

"Enough arguments!" Captain Haran said. "We'll all be lucky to make it through the next few hours. We are surrounded by ships that are likely very hostile to our cause. Any of them could destroy us if we are discovered." She looked at the two of them with an angry frown. "Use this remaining time to consider how you will guarantee this never happens again."

*

Captain Haran, Cal, and Yendos came out of the conference room and went directly to Cal's console on the bridge.

"The only way this happened is if the parameters you gave us were wrong," Cal said. "Or incomplete," he added.

"If you want an explanation, I need to see what you've actually done here. No doubt, you've mangled my principles," Yendos said.

"Operator Heit, log into your console and access the data on the jump into this system," the captain ordered.

Cal sat in the chair. "Look, here it is." He brought the information onscreen.

Yendos leaned in close to the screen. Cal again wondered at the structure of the hood over his face. Clearly, he could see through it somehow.

"I need to see more," Yendos said. "Get out of the chair."

Cal looked back at Yendos and didn't move. "You did this, didn't you? You've intentionally redirected the ship into this system. You could steer us anywhere if you wanted, by feeding us navigation routes only you understand."

"That's ridiculous," Yendos said. "Why would I want to lead you into a pirate sector?"

Councilor Theeran appeared unexpectedly behind Cal. "Operator Heit! Leave your station!" Theeran ordered him.

Cal froze in shock for a moment. Theeran clearly trusted Yendos more than him. Cal got up without a word and walked to the back of the bridge. He watched Yendos sitting in his seat, adjusting the configurations in the navigational computer while explaining the different elements he found to Haran and Theeran. Cal had no way of knowing if Yendos had hidden anything in his upgrades to their navigation data. He'd become certain of one thing: Yendos knew far more about the nature of the transit network than he'd shared with them.

DEFIANT SPACE

*

Leda looked out a window. The rotational gravity of *Fidelity* was always pulling them toward the external hull of the ship, so the viewing portal was on the floor by her feet. She sat cross-legged and gazed down into it. Leda had been staring into the portal, fixated, for most of the past few hours since they'd jumped into the system, gazing at its depths.

Fidelity was crawling through space at an almost dormant level of power. They dared not use their thrusters, any detection systems, or any active listening devices. A ship like *Fidelity* stayed hidden based on the success of its electromagnetic insulation. Nearly all their analytical tools were offline. The last thing the crew wanted to do was to reflect any signals back out into space, though some deflection off the hull was unavoidable. Deactivating all *Fidelity*'s outward signals was simple enough, but other problems remained. With the thruster fully shut down, the reactor was no longer emitting particles from the rear of the ship, but occasional spikes of gamma from the reactor would still escape through the hull. The reactor couldn't be fully shut down and then subsequently restarted in any kind of useful time frame using the equipment available onboard. Bringing the reactor to a low idle state was the best they could achieve. A more serious issue was their infrared heat, produced by their own bodies. Simply the temperature of being alive made them clearly visible in empty space. *Fidelity's* hull, with its ports closed, could trap their thermal energy inside and prevent any heat from escaping into space. The more successfully they hid, the higher the internal temperature would gradually rise until they would eventually be forced to vent heat to survive. That was unavoidable.

Space through the viewing portal was inky black, so opaque that it developed an almost two-dimensional quality. The longer Leda watched, the more white points she could faintly see. *Fidelity* had relatively few transparent windows to outer space, to reduce the obvious risk of breaches in the event of a collision. Any section of the ship with reinforced plastic windows also had valve-sealing doors nearby to close off the area in the event of decompression. Leda was holding a small portable measuring device, able to passively analyze any energy signals it was pointed at. She scanned through the window at each of the points of light in turn, reading what she could about their identity. Some were distant stars, others were planets or moons, and some were large pirate cruisers or smaller interceptor-type vessels passing nearby. Differentiating the vessels from the planets and moons was easy enough, using their much faster relative speed, though any ships at long range appeared stationary. If every planet in the system was surrounded by pirate craft, as it seemed, then most of the pirate vessels would be billions of miles away from them. It made little difference. Although many of the pirates clustered around distant planets, roaming units would occasionally pass nearer their position. The star system they'd entered was so crowded that many moons and asteroids containing reaver ships were still close by.

She tracked a fast-moving white dot. It had to be very near.

Fidelity's only option was to identify as a piece of debris, one of a nearly infinite number, even out in deep, empty interplanetary space. Their ship was at the center of a nest of predators. Some of the largest pirate cruisers she'd observed were almost fifty times *Fidelity*'s mass. They were enormous beasts, perhaps the most frightening warships they'd seen so far, a battleship class, she realized. The whole pirate fleet moved like a swarm of insects, emerging from their hives to buzz through space on a million small errands. Normally, vessels below a certain size struggled to survive in space without the long-term support of a larger ship that kept them supplied with food and oxygen, assuming their pilots had conventional human needs. That wasn't the case here. The quantity of moon bases and asteroid stations in the star system seemed to allow the small ships to operate freely, apart from the usual difficulties of managing acceleration as they traveled across interplanetary distances.

Their transit point, as ever, was at the far end of the solar system. *Fidelity* would need to travel in a circuitous route to avoid any encounters. Their best chance of escape was to approach the transit slowly and quietly.

The solar system around them had been fully colonized, and so the pirates were in full possession of every object in their space. Leda considered how weak their own ship would look to the pirates' eyes, how weak their whole world and culture might seem. The pirates would see themselves as natural predators.

*

Major Rosco surveyed the activity on the bridge, watching as the crew anxiously monitored whether they were remaining undetected. Captain Haran and the offworlder from Allumia were working on some problem at Cal's computer console together. After a while, Captain Haran stepped away to join Rosco.

Rosco stood more alert in the presence of his commanding officer. "Sir. So far, the magnetic dampening unit has successfully kept us hidden from any of the hostile forces in this system."

"We need it to stay that way," Haran said. "We don't have many options otherwise."

Rosco had already considered the possibilities. "If we are identified, given that these ships are known pirate forces, there's a good chance they may try to board and capture us if we're discovered, rather than destroy us outright."

Haran nodded. "Prepare an internal security squad, in case of that. You'll lead them. I've also authorized the full use of weapons within the ship. If the pirates come face-to-face with us on our own ship, then some kind of resistance against them is possible. It's a shame the squad won't have Major Oryx and Major Lee." She became stern. "Tell me what happened during the mission back on the station."

Rosco sighed and put his hands on a railing to lean his weight. For a moment, he struggled to make eye contact. "Lee and Oryx got hit by a plasma grenade. It was quick for them, at least. The blast took them out instantly. I remember only their boots were left, burning."

"What led to that?" Haran asked.

"We got involved in a shoot-out on our way back out of the scrapyard. Knocking out the electric power to the area was a good distraction, but it didn't last long enough for us to escape."

"The generator was shut down for your team, just as the plan required," Haran said.

"Well, it came back online while we were still in there," Rosco said. "And we didn't waste any time. They must have spotted us on cameras as soon as the power came back. They came straight for us."

"How did the civilians perform?"

Rosco exhaled and nodded. "They did well. They didn't panic. I owe my life to them, actually. They didn't exactly follow my orders, but they were a key part of the mission's success. They handled all the technical aspects perfectly. I selected them mainly for being among the most fit and healthy of the engineering and science departments, but they performed well under fire."

"Then keep an eye on those two," Haran said. "We may need them again. Make sure they can be relied on to act appropriately in an emergency."

Rosco nodded.

"The plasma grenade you saw…" Haran said. "Did you get any sense of whether they were common?"

Rosco considered. "I expect they had at least a few more. They seemed quite willing to use it. Potentially, there's a lot of ordinance in the interior of that space station, really. It must be unsafe."

"We observed numerous Universal Legion ships above Paxis Prime in our short time docked in orbit. It seems they'll be present at every metropolitan planet we arrive at. Did you leave anything that could identify us as from Vale Reach?" she asked.

"No."

"Are you certain?"

"Yes," he said. "Our identity is safe."

They were quiet for a moment.

"I'm still thinking about what could be done against something like that grenade," Rosco said.

Captain Haran patted him on the shoulder. "Oryx and Lee are our first casualties. I would pray they'll be our only casualties, but I'm not able to believe something like that." She shook her head. "I'll prepare a dossier for you on the kinds of extreme weapons we could encounter on missions: plasma explosives, rail guns, flechettes, acid weapons. It's all nasty stuff. If it hits anyone, there's almost no chance to survive."

"We have body armor in the armory. Should we make the heavy plating standard issue for expeditions?" Rosco asked.

"Our armor is cardboard against a plasma grenade," she said. "Those kinds of weapons aren't meant for us. That's what we should be concerned about. No one builds a portable weapon that powerful unless they've got some tough nuts to crack. It demonstrates what's out there. Someone needs a blast that intense to put them down."

"Every culture has legends of super-powered beings. We've all heard the tales," he said.

"So far, it looks to be true," Haran said.

*

Leda was inside the engineering workshop on *Fidelity*, working alone. On the table in front of her was a complex assortment of flasks, vials, and machinery made of metal and glass. Positioned farther back on the desk were two huge distillation vats. Already, she was seeing wondrous things. Chemical structures were forming in ways she'd never seen before. She was experimenting on samples taken from the atmosphere of Allumia while she'd been down on the planet's surface. There were molecules in the mixture that no one from Vale Reach had ever observed. The development of new fuels was progressing better than she'd allowed herself to hope for.

Leda had more material to review than she'd probably get through in a lifetime. She took a long metal probe and inserted it into one of the vials of liquid then read the results off a small screen.

As she watched the flow of numbers and figures, Leda felt as if she was gaining entry to some exclusive club that had been denied to anyone from Vale Reach. These findings from beyond just their own planet were a new beginning.

Leda suddenly became aware that someone was behind her. "Holy fuck!" She spun around.

A figure in an enormous black hooded body suit was standing close behind her, holding a long length of string. It looked like Yendos, but it wasn't. It was Ontu, the assistant, she realized.

"What the hell are you doing?" she demanded.

It was a measuring tape he held in his hand.

"I'm sorry." Ontu looked down at the ground in disappointment, and his shoulders sagged slightly.

"What are you doing?" she demanded again.

"Yendos gave me a task. He wants me to collect measurements of you all, but I have to do it very respectfully. We're not trying to cause any offense to anyone. You seemed so focused on what you were doing, I thought it was a good time to record your height."

Leda was startled by how nonsensical his answer was. "Why are you measuring me? I'm going to need a proper answer to that question."

His hands waved as he explained. "We want to measure all the people of Vale Reach! You may be vital to our research. We're using your ship's crew as a sample to estimate what the whole population must be like."

Leda folded her arms. "What research?"

Ontu raised his arms in a pleading gesture. He hesitated. "It's at a sensitive stage. You can't ask us to share our ongoing notes. You're a technologist yourself—you must understand that. The risk of our life's work being stolen is too great."

Leda understood the feeling. Perhaps she would do the same thing in their position.

"Get out of here, Ontu," she said. "And don't measure me again."

*

The time was late at night by the ship's internal clock. The lights were dimmed and yellow. Cal was hurrying wearily to reach his bunk after the end of a long shift. He wanted to take off his uniform and forget about everything. He turned a corner at a junction and collided with Rosco. Cal stumbled and fell to the floor.

"Oh god, I'm sorry." Rosco reached down and lifted Cal to his feet.

A little dazed, Cal responded slowly. "It's fine. Don't worry about it."

Rosco waited a moment. "You know, Cal, I've been thinking. I need to apologize to you for taking you and Leda into that scrapyard. You guys came under direct fire, and I never expected that to happen. It was a serious risk you took, and... maybe I didn't do a proper job of warning you how bad it would be. Maybe I sort of pushed you into it. I'm sorry for that."

Cal was surprised for a moment. Rosco was right—the events at the scrap heap had been incredibly stressful. Cal hadn't been sleeping much since. But as he looked into Rosco's sincere eyes, he found it impossible to be angry. Rosco was faced with an impossible task. He had to save all of Vale Reach. To some degree, Cal shared that task as well, but Cal also definitely had to keep himself alive if he was going to return to Eevey one day.

He patted Rosco on the shoulder. "It's fine. Really. We all have to work together on this."

"Thanks," Rosco said. "That's really good of you."

Rosco had been listening to music on headphones, which had fallen to the floor, and Cal reached down to pick them up. The sound of unearthly singing could be heard emitting loudly from the headphones.

"That's kind of intense," Cal said as he handed them back to Rosco.

"It's folk music from Vale Reach," Rosco said. "I found it in the archives onboard. Just think"—he sounded more reflective than usual—"if we're too late and we come back to find Vale Reach is destroyed, this song would be all that remained of its kind. We'd be the last people to ever remember it. The only trace of our society ever existing would be the people in this ship." He went quiet.

Cal hadn't seen him in such low spirits before. He seemed filled with desperation and deep existential fear.

"Not if you can prevent disaster from occurring, Major," Cal said sincerely. "I sleep better knowing you're monitoring the situation."

Rosco smiled and closed his eyes for a brief second. "Thank you. I appreciate your optimism."

"Good night, Major Rosco," Cal said.

They continued their separate ways down the corridor.

Chapter 10

The transit point was in sight. Leda watched from her seat on the bridge as *Fidelity* approached the target. They would cross its threshold in under twenty minutes. The star system around them still simmered with the same degree of constant low-level activity as when they'd first arrived. None of the pirate ships had been disturbed from their regular activities. The network of asteroid bases and satellite stations showed no change. Somehow, the tension on the bridge only seemed to grow as the moment of escape approached. Everyone waited at their stations in anxious anticipation.

Suddenly, many signals launched as Leda watched in horror. It was exactly what they'd been dreading. The screens of *Fidelity*'s bridge reported dozens of pirate vessels abruptly changing path. Other ships appeared in the empty void where they'd been hiding in a lower-power state. *Fidelity* was surrounded from every angle. They would be intercepted no matter what evasive maneuvers they took, even factoring in any enhanced fuels in their turning engines. *Fidelity* began to fully power up its reactor again, as the time for subterfuge was over. Leda doubted they had many options in terms of escape or combat, but at least the ship would have all systems operational.

"Weapons fire!" a member of bridge crew called out.

A sense of fear spread through the bridge, as though the atmosphere was electrified.

"We've registered an energy spike. Looks to be a rail gun launch."

Ahead, a pirate frigate orbiting a moon close by the transit point had discharged a massive weapon, likely a railgun.

Leda's heart raced. A large railgun shot could tear their ship in half, but over such a long distance, the shot would not arrive for minutes. Leda focused on her screen and tried not to panic. The crew had to keep to their duties no matter the danger. Their actions in a time of catastrophe mattered more than at any other time. Leda told herself like a mantra that following protocol was the safest route, even as her hands were shaking.

"Get us away from the projectile's path," Captain Haran said.

The ship weaved and swayed as the turning engines tried to rapidly move *Fidelity* out from the target zone.

"The projectile is separating," Cal reported from his console. A railgun shot between ships could separate into a cluster of projectiles, filling the target space with a spray of ultra-high-velocity shrapnel. "It's separating apart so much," Cal said. "I'm getting anomalous signal reflections back from it. It might not be a solid object anymore. It's expanded too much to be built for kinetic damage."

They'd run out of time. The strike was imminent.

"All crew brace for impact!" Captain Haran shouted.

Every crew member on *Fidelity* grabbed hold of something solid and held on for their life.

The ship rocked as it was hit. Crew were thrown violently up into the air. The ship's interior had been built with round surfaces for just such an eventuality. Leda managed to stay strapped into her seat. She checked her systems. No hull breaches were registered.

"Damage reports," demanded Captain Haran.

The ship was still intact. Most stations reported no damage.

"All maneuvering engines along one side are jammed," one crewman said.

Motors and power conduits on a single side of the ship were all reporting anomalies, Leda saw.

"The ship's movement is changing," said another crewman. "It's like something is impeding us. We're decelerating fast."

Leda couldn't make sense of what was happening.

"Give me external visual displays of the affected side," Haran said.

The main screen came to life. Some shiny silver structure covered most of *Fidelity*'s exterior. It was recognizable as a kind of net that glistened under the glow of the electric lamps on *Fidelity*'s outer surface. The silver material appeared gelatinous, almost like thick glue in long strands. The camera panned around. Leda saw that one long enormous strand of the net reached far back out into space, seeming to reach an infinite distance back out in the blackness. Leda realized why they hadn't been destroyed. They'd been immobilized, prepared for capture. She studied the structure of the largest strand. *Fidelity* reflected radio signals up and down its length. It reached for millions of kilometers.

"We need to remove this immediately. Someone find a way to untangle the ship," Captain Haran ordered.

Most of the bridge looked back at her without any ideas.

"We could send out an external team in void suits to cut away at it," Leda suggested.

"Engineering division, begin assembling an external team for hull repairs." Haran sent the command throughout the ship.

"I can see a pirate ship approaching the strand," Cal reported.

The whole ship lurched again, many people being shaken from their feet by the unexpected shove. The shove became a constant pull in one direction. *Fidelity* was being carried away.

"The pirate vessel's taken hold of the long strand, and they're pulling us completely off course," Cal reported.

The pirates knew exactly what they were doing, Leda thought. They'd completed this process many times before, while the crew of *Fidelity* could only guess at what came next. Leda suddenly realized a terrible problem.

"We're getting more entangled, Captain!" she said. "Each time *Fidelity* rotates, the fiber strand wraps completely around the hull. We've already become deeply tangled by it. Our artificial gravity is causing us to become further enveloped."

"Reverse the rotational gravity engines," Haran ordered. "Get us to zero rotation immediately."

After a few seconds, the crew felt their weight disappear and their feet lose contact with the floor. People's hair drifted around them. Leda kept one hand on a railing and one foot in a gap beneath her desk to keep herself anchored in position in zero gravity. The other crew did the same.

"Use the main nuclear thruster to pull us back away from the net," Haran said.

That was a brute force approach, but it was worth trying. The crew increased the nuclear thruster to full power. The ship began to shake more violently than they'd ever felt before.

"The strand is stretching," Leda said, "but it's not breaking. It's pulling back at us with a lot of elastic force. It's still stuck tightly to the hull. It's an adhesive. Tension is high. I'm recording structural stress across the whole ship. The support beams are beginning to stretch."

If the fiber didn't snap, *Fidelity* would rip itself apart. A creaking began to be audible, becoming loud even within the bridge.

"Reduce the engine power," Haran said. "Don't cause damage to the ship." She was angry and frustrated. "Report on the other pirate ships. Where are they?"

"They now seem positioned to observe us," Cal said. "They're maintaining a steady distance."

"We have to assume they're taking us to a specific location," Haran said.

Leda studied what she could about the ship towing them. It had begun to wind in the long filament like a fishing line. From their direction of travel, she saw *Fidelity* was being taken toward an enormous cluster of asteroids near the center of the system. A quiet murmur set in across the bridge as the crew tried to devise any method of escape. Before long, two small starships quickly came up to the external hull of *Fidelity* and clamped themselves to the ship using mechanical arms. The noises were heard throughout the interior of their vessel. The small ships activated their engines, burning at immensely high temperatures, and *Fidelity* accelerated along a new path.

After several hours of travel, they arrived at a vast asteroid field, which they entered, weaving between the colossal rocks. The two small ships clamped to their exterior were controlling *Fidelity*'s movement entirely. Their sensors showed the asteroids around them on all sides were crawling with pirate vessels and settlements. Leda detected that the lead vessel had released its connection to the filament strand that entangled them. Soon, *Fidelity* arrived at the largest and most imposing asteroid of the entire cluster. A fortress filled its surface.

Its image filled *Fidelity*'s bridge screen. Despite her oppressive terror, Leda felt thrilled as she looked at the monstrous construct. Finally, they'd found something unimaginably powerful in scale and size. As she'd always feared, they would likely be swiftly destroyed by their discovery. The asteroid base reached out so wide in front of them that it resembled a planet in their view. The gray rocks around were the raw building blocks that all worlds were made from, left over from the creation of the planets. The rays of a sun struck the rear of its surface, causing it to glow brightly at its edges and casting impenetrable black shadows deep into its surface. Ranges of sharp mountains stretched up high in every direction. The dusty gray of its natural surface contrasted with the black metal structures encrusting it, like algae crawling across a stone.

Most of the buildings and towers were heavy and solid, like a citadel made of iron. As they drew nearer, the rolling, jagged mountain ranges and metal spires stretching away in every direction made the asteroid base resemble some kind of titanic sea clam. Leda saw tiny windows like pricks of light, numbering in the thousands, across every side of each tower. Wrecked and burnt starships hung suspended in chains between the towers, like flies in a spider web a hundred kilometers wide. Flags and banners adorned the structures. The largest had to be monumental in length. The banners were positioned facing outward to greet any arrivals, and Leda saw on their surface great leering skulls, the universal symbol for death.

The ship was approaching a huge natural gateway into the structure. Inside the opening, the asteroid had sponge-like cavities that had been filled by the black metal machinery of human settlements. The two vessels on their surface pulled them farther onward. *Fidelity* entered a deep hole in the rock, a dark crevasse awaiting them like a mouth hungry to swallow up ships. As they passed inside, the last traces of starlight disappeared. With a jolt, the ship came to a halt in a massive docking area.

Leda watched on the ship's external cameras as a metal portcullis closed across the gateway they'd entered from. No sound was transmitted though the vacuum. She checked the other external cameras. The two small ships clamped to *Fidelity's* surface remained attached, but they'd powered down their engines. Dozens of other starships were in the same docking area, connected to the asteroid's interior by pipes and cables. Leda and the rest of the bridge crew assessed everything they could see around them. Most of the docked vessels looked to be pirate ships, carrying large, obvious weapons and armor plating on their surfaces. Others were civilian ships of various kinds, many of them battered and burnt with patches of damage. Leda saw tiny signs of movement across every ship. Small teams of workers were flying through the empty space, carrying tools or welding surfaces with small bright flashes of light. Leda saw countless gates and valves in the rock around them. From one, a metal tube emerged, wriggling through the silence like a worm. It seemed to bite into the side of *Fidelity*. Throughout the interior of the ship, the crew heard the grinding sound of it forming an airtight seal.

"A boarding pipe has made contact!" Leda said.

"Major Rosco, lead the internal security squad to the point of entry," Captain Haran said.

*

Rosco watched as an orange ring of heat two meters in diameter appeared in the side of the hull. Theoretically, it was being cut into the floor beneath their feet, but without gravity, that ceased to be relevant. The boarding pipe outside seemed able to melt its way through.

"Couldn't they have found an entrance port?" Rosco muttered to himself.

Major Rosco and eight other soldiers comprised the security team. They'd consulted with Advocate Fargas while the ship was being impounded. Fargas had recommended a policy of compliance. That went against Rosco's instincts, but he could see the reasoning. They could attempt to fight the pirates in *Fidelity*'s corridors, but given the potential volume of opponents they faced, that would only guarantee a violent death. An attempt at cooperation was their only path to survival.

The security team waited, facing the wide glowing ring where the boarding pipe was breaching the hull. They kept far back from the heat of whatever was cutting through the metal, and their weapons stayed holstered. Rosco had issued the extra-thick body armor, despite Haran's advice otherwise.

Rosco's heart beat loud and fast until he felt the pressure like a burning in his nerves.

The glowing ring of metal suddenly lurched backward, removing a disc of metal from the hull of the ship. The atmosphere from inside the boarding tube came in with a damp mold-like smell. The metal disc was rotated ninety degrees out of position, and they were face-to-face with the pirates.

Rosco could see around a dozen, both men and women, within the tube. Most looked disinterested though the ones at the front of the group were ready for action. Three pirates carried guns, while the tallest at the front carried two shining silver knives. Most of them wore some kind of small breathing apparatus around their chest and neck, and underneath, they wore body suits all brightly patterned in different colors. Most had lean human musculature visible through their form-fitting outfits, but others had stranger shapes, revealing that parts of their original bodies had been replaced. They paused at the sight of Rosco and the security squad.

Rosco stared at the thick barrels of their guns. "I am Major Rosco, representative of the bridge staff of this ship. You are trespassing aboard our vessel."

The lead pirate seemed to consider him for a moment, as well as the rest of the security team. He then gestured softly for the other pirates to lower their guns. He smoothly floated onto the ship and came directly up to Rosco, stopping by placing a toe on the floor. He was much taller than Rosco had realized but also thin. His leanness seemed artificial, as though all traces of fat had been sucked out of him. Fluorescent-green-and-pink checker patterns covered his body. He had no body hair, though he had dark black eyebrows and long, almost equine facial features. His skin was pale, likely from lack of

UV, but with darker patches of almost black. Only his face was exposed.

He grabbed one of Rosco's arms and twisted it so that Rosco was forced to turn around. Other security squad members reacted in alarm, but they didn't intervene. Rosco still had his pistol at his waist, but the pirate seemed unconcerned. With an enormous knife still held in one hand, the pirate gestured toward the main door out of that section of the ship. This man wouldn't hesitate to kill them all if needed, Rosco sensed. Perhaps it would be possible to prevent bloodshed among the crew. The pirate pushed Rosco toward the door, his arm still twisted behind him. Rosco hesitated to enter the code to open the door. Perhaps he could delay their arrival at the bridge, giving the crew more time to analyze the invaders. The pirate jabbed him a few times with the tip of the knife. It was sharp like a needle and passed straight through his armor and clothes. Rosco opened the door.

Behind them, the rest of the pirate crew came aboard. They pushed the security team along in front of them and confiscated the weapons from each officer.

*

The door to the bridge opened, revealing Major Rosco and the pirates.

The bridge crew looked up from their consoles in shock, forty faces from both above and below in the cylindrical bridge, including Councilor Theeran, Captain Haran, and all the other officers at their stations. The *Fidelity* crew were motionless in uncertainty.

Rosco and the pirate leader floated in through the doorway to the bridge, and all the other pirates entered the bridge behind them. A state of heightened tension began as the two groups sized each other up in the zero-gravity environment.

Captain Haran came forward toward them. "I am the captain of this ship."

The pirates watched her. They understood what she said. Rosco watched from a powerless position as one quickly floated straight towards Haran, passing over crew at their consoles. The pirate took a set of handcuffs from a pouch in their outfit and swiftly applied them to Captain Haran. At a signal from the pirate leader, the other pirates went around the bridge to similarly restrain the rest of the bridge crew. After a moment, they paused in confusion and looked at each other, uncertain what to do. They hadn't brought anywhere near enough pairs of handcuffs. The pirates seemed perplexed by how many people made up the bridge crew of *Fidelity*.

The pirate leader released Rosco from his grip and floated slowly around, examining the bridge more closely, checking various features and shaking his head. Rosco had been placed in handcuffs already. The pirate leader seemed to abruptly run out of patience or curiosity and waved for the rest of the pirates to get the crew off the bridge. Half of the pirates pushed all the handcuffed prisoners forward, while the rest remained on the bridge.

The bridge crew were taken through *Fidelity* to where the boarding tube had breached the side of the vessel. None of them could move easily through the zero-gravity environment with their hands bound, so they were thrown down the corridors by the pirates like large bundles. On the way to the portal, Rosco met Marraz being led along by another pirate.

"Let's hope these guys are in a charitable mood," he told Rosco.

They left the ship and entered the boarding tube. Rosco smelled damp air from earlier return. It swiftly grew stronger, becoming a stench as they exited the tube into the asteroid itself. The interior was dark, with just a handful of very dim lamps to light the way. The noises of industry echoed through the corridors, banging and hammering that sounded as though it came from many locations all around. The asteroid had no gravity, just as *Fidelity* had none once their rotational motion had shut down. Being weightless, each crewman was easily pushed along by a pirate. Other pirates passed by them within the corridors of the asteroid, seemingly going about their business. None of them gave the *Fidelity* crew a second glance. Some wore the same bright outfits as the pirates who'd captured their vessel, but others wore simpler, less ostentatious suits. Everyone Rosco saw looked taller than any of the *Fidelity* crew.

The corridors were dark and winding. His high stress levels made it hard for Rosco to accurately judge the passage of time. They traveled past a series of immense open doorways. Through them, Rosco briefly saw an enormous hangar bay. Hundreds of voidcraft, maybe thousands, were arranged in rows, with a series of long mechanical arms that brought equipment to each craft. Farther away rested a voidcraft far larger than any they'd seen before, roughly half the length of *Fidelity*. He was amazed. Voidcraft could only operate with the logistical support of a proper starship to bring them to battle and keep them loaded with ammunition. The engines on these super-heavy gunships were designed for maneuvers rather than acceleration. The entire fleet of attack craft stretched on inside the asteroid for what looked like infinity. The total firepower was devastating. Whoever controlled the facilities here could surely threaten any imaginable adversary. Given the size of the asteroid base they'd observed, he was seeing only one hangar bay of many.

They progressed on, deeper into the barely lit tunnels of the asteroid. The pirates must have powerful low-light vision to work comfortably in the dim environment, Rosco thought. Suddenly, he heard human moans from the passageways ahead of them, cries of suffering that made his hairs stand on end. He looked around, desperately trying to see what was coming. He could see only the walls of powdery gray stone. Rosco's hand brushed against their rough surface as he moved along.

The screams suddenly became louder as they drew closer to the source. They had entered dungeons, he realized. They were passing by the doors to cells, each with bars across a small window. At times, they would reach an open cavity that showed Rosco thousands more cells filling the interior on all sides. In zero gravity, those cavities could be crossed easily. The corridor around them vanished, and they floated ahead through a wide empty space. The number of cells Rosco saw became uncountable, many tens of thousands, at least. Flickers of dim electric light glinted across the bars of the endless cages. The pirates and their prisoners entered a new section of corridor, and the environment around them became dark again.

The cries of pain were sudden and nearer. Each cell Rosco passed was small like a coffin, barely larger than a single person, maintaining isolation for the prisoner. The long corridors themselves had been designed to reverberate sound, like the pipes of an acoustic organ, he saw. The screams resonated and amplified from every hard, flat surface till the sound washed over them in deafening, pulsating waves. The prisoners' cries echoed, until the entire prison functioned as a deranged musical instrument. It could only have been intentionally built that way. A lunatic designed this place, Rosco realized, someone with a natural affinity for creating nightmares. They passed a few larger cells, from which he heard spoken voices and the crackle of electricity as the sounds of pain grew even louder. The torture chambers were interwoven with the small holding cells so that the screams from the punishment could clearly reach everyone imprisoned throughout the dungeon decks. One pirate floated out from a room, casually smoking a pipe. He nodded in nonchalant greeting to the pirates carrying the *Fidelity* crew along. The noise around them was bloodcurdling, like an agony without end, turning the dark corners of the asteroid into a howling blackness full of terror.

Finally, the corridor widened, and the stonework around them became less rough in design. The passageways in the area they entered had been carved smooth and symmetrical, unlike the outer areas. Rosco wasn't sure if the light had grown any brighter or if his eyes had adapted to the confined environment. The group stopped. In front of them was a series of gates of black metal, like dark iron, covered in spikes and barbs. On either side of the first gate were flags and banners, like miniature versions of those they'd seen outside in space. A keypad was mounted in the wall, and the lead pirate entered a code. With a loud grinding, each piece of the thick metal gate retracted, one after the other, until an open space beckoned them. Rosco and the other crew were taken inside.

Chapter 11

The crew of the *Fidelity* were in the center of a regal courtroom, displayed like an exhibit. Cal felt hundreds of pairs of eyes looking at them. Pirates stood frozen mid-conversation as though interrupted by the *Fidelity* crew's arrival. They seemed separated into different groups. Some wore fur pelts of strange animals around their shoulders. Others had shiny chrome plating covering their bodies or patterns of scars visible across their naked chests. In zero gravity, they appeared at every orientation, some upside down, some standing horizontally against a wall. Cal saw no convention as to what was ceiling and floor. The upside-down faces were deeply unsettling, grinning and sneering in cruel disdain. Cal could see all genders and all ages, too, judging from the small height of some of them. He spotted what looked like a five-year-old twirling a fluorescent machete. He quickly looked away as the child glared angrily at him.

Cal looked around behind him and realized he'd failed to register the most important thing in the huge room. A raised platform sat at the chamber's center, a dais of many levels that dominated the court. The chamber was a throne room, Cal realized, and seated on the throne was a king.

The man's inhuman face seized all his attention—Cal had initially blocked it out in shock, but now he realized the man was not wearing any mask but in fact had the mouth of a demon. It was a gigantic mouth, nearly twice the width of the rest of the man's already large skull, and circular, with lips like a fish. The teeth were triangular and serrated like a saw. A black tongue wriggled out from between the teeth, as though tasting the air. Several more black tongues emerged from the same mouth, and Cal instinctively tried to jump back a small distance. The man was the largest person Cal had ever seen, perhaps fifteen feet tall if he were to stand. Instead, the figure sat cross-legged, hovering in the air a few inches above his throne. He didn't drift even slightly. His outfit appeared to be some kind of hardened leather bodysuit on which images of people had been hand-painted, like murals on a wall.

Their original captors arranged them in a horizontal line before the throne as the fanged giant watched. He seemed to be grinning, but his face had not yet moved in any way, and his monstrous features made his emotions difficult to read. His sitting posture was more instructive, suggesting curiosity, perhaps even amusement, like the other occupants in the room.

One of the king's courtiers drifted forward, a shriveled-looking man who wore a flowing silk robe and had an additional pair of hands where his feet should've been. He crossed the room toward them and gurgled a series of commands in an expectant tone. To Cal's surprise, Advocate Fargas spoke up in response from their midst. The *Fidelity* crew backed away from him slightly as Fargas and the courtier exchanged dialogue. Then Fargas turned around toward the rest of the crew.

"So they're looking for someone to, uh, to be interviewed. They have a few questions," he said.

"Understandably, they're aware something about you just doesn't make sense."

Councilor Theeran stepped forward. "I am the representative of us all. I will answer on our behalf."

The giant on the throne shook his head, and the crew froze in shock. That was the first movement he'd made since they entered the room. The giant snapped his fingers, emitting a thunderous crack, then pointed directly at Cal. Two pirates grabbed Cal by each arm and carried him farther toward the throne. It was the last place he wanted to go. Cal felt visceral revulsion and panic. He tried not to squirm as he was brought forward, where he could smell the giant man. It was a strange smell to identify—alien, he realized with shock, a chemical code not part of organic life as his senses could instinctively recognize it. The giant in the throne was unmistakably staring directly down at him.

Behind Cal, Fargas stepped forward and began talking. After a moment of back and forth between Fargas and the courtier, Fargas hurried up to Cal's side.

"I've persuaded them to let me assist you as legal counsel and as your translator. It's a privileged position, even here. You can thank me later." Fargas slapped Cal on the back reassuringly. "Remember to keep up a confident face. Look optimistic. Maybe even a little clueless. Don't feel guilty. Don't look like someone who could cause any sort of difficult issue."

The courtier in the silk robe gurgled something else at Cal.

Fargas whispered into his ear again. "Okay, first question: Do you know who this is?" He nodded slightly toward the throne.

Cal looked confused then terrified. "Is that the question?"

"I'll tell him you don't." Fargas then spoke to the courtier, and a ripple of laughter echoed around the room.

More people were filing into the back of the room, Cal realized. They'd attracted an audience.

"Okay, so his name—well, it's more of a title really—it's... how you would say it is 'Lizard King.' But you've got to put the emphasis on Lizard. It's *Lizard* King. He likes that. So say it right. The irony is he looks more like a frog."

"Okay." Cal started to shake.

"Okay, next question," Fargas said. He took another gurgled message from the advisor. "Is this your first time meeting real pirates? I think the King is trying to ease you in gently."

"Oh," Cal said. "That's good of him. Right?"

The Lizard King laughed out loud suddenly, a slow, full-throated laugh, then spoke directly. "Do you know... most crews immediately self-destruct when they meet us?"

His lips moved quickly, flashing to form complex shapes around his massive teeth, but his voice had a surprisingly clear accent. He was able to sound close to a normal human.

"They overload their reactor and end things quickly. It's an annoyance, really. We have our tools to prevent this, the grappling nets and so on, but until we can fully constrain their reactor with magnetic clamps, there always remains a window for it to be possible. Most successful suicides take place at the first moment we begin our interception. You are, of course, far past that point now."

"Oh," Cal said. "Yes, I can see that we are."

"But you didn't take that chance," the Lizard King said.

"No," Cal said. He tried to sound certain and nodded as though it had all been intentional. He remembered the moment and how none of them had considered such a course of action.

"The moment passed you by. Perhaps you lacked situational awareness. Perhaps that lack of awareness could help you now. We're not the worst people in space, you know. There isn't an obligation to self-destruct when you meet us! So many do, of course, but I always say that's more reflective of them than of me."

Cal nodded in agreement without fully comprehending why. "That sounds reasonable. I agree with that."

"You made a decision without thinking, without realizing you even had. It's an unspoken decision that's always with us, like a worm at the bottom of a pool. Only when everything else is drained out does it become visible. Tell me, do you still stand by your choice to face me alive? Or would you commit suicide right now if I granted you the opportunity? Would you rather we conduct our conversation in the mortuary, beyond the veil of death?" The Lizard King opened his bulbous eyes wide. "Or shall we find another fate for you?"

Cal stammered as his mind went blank. He felt like he could hear the screaming from the prison decks again though that had to be his imagination. He felt as though his eyes were shaking, just like his hands were, till the whole universe rattled.

"My client does not have to answer that question," Fargas said.

The Lizard King waved a hand at him. It had three thumbs and very many fingers. "Your advocate serves you well. I wonder how you came to have him. If you have chosen life, then there will be a toll. It begins with answers. You are not a freighter. You are certainly not Palladian."

"You should ask our captain. She has all these answers," Cal said.

"I like to hear from the common man," the Lizard King said. "I think it's important to always understand the perspective of things at ground level."

"Okay. Well… we're on a journey," Cal said.

The Lizard King put his hands together. "Good. I love a journey. You can be on your way, then."

"Oh," Cal breathed out in relief. "Really?"

"Not at all! You've entered into my territory. My territory! That's an act of trespassing. I need restitution from you."

"We didn't mean to. We're trying to reach the Ruarken Senate."

From behind him, Cal heard Councilor Theeran calling for him to be quiet, but the sound was very distant.

The Lizard King's eyebrows raised to the top of his head. Cal didn't realize he even had eyebrows till they started moving. After a few seconds of pause, the Lizard King spoke again. "Are you certain you're on the right path? Ruarken isn't anywhere near here. Perhaps you should flay your navigator."

Cal laughed nervously. "I mean, technically, I would be the…" Cal stopped. "No, someone else gave me the jump parameters. I didn't bring us here."

"And who did?" the Lizard King inquired.

Cal froze for a moment. "Yendos."

The Lizard King snapped his fingers again, a thunderous crack. "Bring up Yendos," he called.

"Wait," Cal said, "I didn't mean for…"

Yendos was dragged forward from the group of prisoners and brought to stand next to Cal. Yendos turned to stare coldly at Cal, who could feel his hostility though the black hood, as ever.

"Shit," Cal said. "I'm sorry for getting you up here."

"I can assure you, my lord," Yendos told the Lizard King, "I have the utmost respect for your authority, and I would never be part of any mistaken entry into your territory."

The Lizard King frowned, his large eyebrows coming back down. "Well, it seems like it's no one's at fault, then, doesn't it?" He turned to his advisors. "Sell them. Sell the ship too. Sell everything. To the usual people."

The pirates immediately began to drag the *Fidelity* crew away. The crew panicked as they realized what was happening. Some kicked and fought back, but they were ineffective in zero gravity with their hands bound. The pirates carried them back toward the barbed black iron gateway. A metallic grinding sounded as the door slowly opened again. Everyone was shouting in anger and fear, with Haran and Theeran appealing to anyone who would listen. The court watched with impassive amusement.

"Wait!" shouted Cal. "I have valuable information to share with you! I have important secrets! Bring them back!"

The Lizard King made a noise, and his pirates stopped removing *Fidelity*'s crew. "Go on. Settle some wagers amongst the courtiers. Tell us where you're really from."

"We're from a planet called Vale Reach," Cal said.

The Lizard King was pleased. "And tell me… why did you leave that little place? Make it something I want to hear."

Cal looked around. Everyone was staring at him, all the members of court and all the crew of *Fidelity*. He cleared his throat and continued. "I'm pretty sure our planet is fucked." Cal looked back at Councilor Theeran and shrugged in a guilty and apologetic way. "Sorry… but…" He turned back to the Lizard King. "If I'm totally honest, I think it may already be too late for Vale Reach. The Universal Legion is claiming our planet."

The Lizard King scowled disapprovingly for a moment. "How unfortunate."

"You've met them?" Cal asked.

The Lizard King seemed to intensify his perpetual, shark-like smile. "Do you think I have?"

"So they're no friends of yours either, then? That's something we have in common," Cal said.

"They're hated by everyone. You think the Ruarken will save you?"

Cal shook his head. "I have no idea. I'm not sure if I honestly believe anything will stop the Legion. It feels like the key decisions have been made already, you know? People claim there's a system of laws and procedures out there, but I think those with power just do whatever they want and make up excuses later."

"I know exactly what you mean," the Lizard King said. "But your mission to Ruarken is absurd. You stand no chance."

"I know," Cal said. "But to us, this is the end of our lives. To the Legion, we're probably just a number on a spreadsheet. We can't quit. Once our planet is theirs, it'll never return to us. You don't have to be a genius to know the ways imperial occupations hold onto power or what happens when a foreign people become just a resource or an inconvenience. It's all happened many times before. So we have no choice." Cal looked down at his own hands. "We're going to the Ruarken Senate, or we'll die trying. Apparently, the Ruarken are sane and reasonable people who'll put a stop to the Legion's annexation, though even that's just what someone else has told us."

"Because all of the people who wouldn't fight the Universal Legion on your behalf were just being completely unreasonable..." the Lizard King said sarcastically. "Continue. This is the most refreshing take our court has received in a while."

"That's kind of my point, though. Are we meant to just sit back and be bullied? That's hopeless. People can't live without hope. They're not built that way. No one is. So if everything that happens in this universe is all determined by raw power... then we need to get ourselves some."

The Lizard King clapped his hands in satisfaction. "Magnificently reasoned. This is gold. You've got balls, you little people. You're absolutely brave. Legendary, perhaps, in terms of your ambition. You're just going to ask the Ruarken Senate to demand the Legion calls the whole thing off?"

Fargas stepped forward and interjected. "We're going to model ourselves as the perfect test case for the Ruarken Senate to assert its willingness not to be intimidated by the Universal Legion."

The Lizard King grinned and slapped his knee, which caused him to slowly rotate in the zero gravity. "So your next destination is…?"

"The Grand Highway at Thelmia would be our next target, your majesty," Fargas said.

"Terrific." The Lizard King suddenly pointed at Marraz. "I recognize you."

All eyes turned toward Marraz, who looked at the floor as though embarrassed slightly. "I guess you might."

"You've been pirating these shipping lanes with Tarufa's crew for several years now. A violent crew, as I recall. You were a unique one. From some backwater by the name of…" He slapped his other knee suddenly, and stopped spinning. "Vale Reach! So that's why you're with these idiots!" He chuckled, a deep belly laugh again. "You're babysitting these ignorant bumpkins on their mad journey. My god. How much are they paying you?"

"They aren't," Marraz said.

The Lizard King howled, both in laughter and despair. "Gods alive! Charity work. What a nightmare. Your ship's probably not even worth stripping for parts. What is the value of this fake freighter?"

The king's advisor drifted to the base of the throne and passed up a large, flat datapad. The Lizard King scrolled it casually with a swipe of his thumb. An absolute silence began that seemed to grow heavy in the air. Eventually, the Lizard King looked up from the datapad, his bulbous eyes rotating. He rubbed his rows of teeth together, their serrated edges creating a rapid clicking against each other. Cal saw the calculation in his eyes.

"Do you want to know how I got these teeth?" he asked Cal.

Cal hesitated, like a deer in the headlights. "Yes," he croaked after a moment. "Yes, tell me."

"I was a young man, not so different from you, living aboard a frigate in the Karnelik Depths. My place was in the gunnery platforms, where I would watch as vessels broke open and burst when we struck them. I was excellent at it. My rail cannon could split a ship's decks from bow to stern without putting a scratch on the cargo. Later on, of course, the bounties of the Depths became slim. Then there was just the gangs and nothing but each other. We began pushing into new territory. One cycle, we became ambushed by Xenological raiders, a perfect ambush, dozens of strike craft emerging from hiding. Have you heard of the Xeno?"

Cal had heard of them. Everyone had, on some basic level. Such a primal concept managed to travel via an almost unexplainable word of mouth—an alien.

"I remember them breaking into our deck. Our gun was still killing their comrades out in space, you see, so we were an urgent priority. I remember slimy hands in a crushing grip around me, like a vice with so very many fingers, wet like the tentacles of an octopus. I bit out the Xeno's throat with my original teeth." The Lizard King leaned forward and waited a moment. "I took a chunk of his neck, the biggest I could fit in my mouth, chomping down on whatever windpipe he had in there. I remember the spray, the spurt of putrid fluids that erupted from him, the taste. As you can see"—he stroked his fingers over his black lips—"his blood left me with a gift to remember him by. It seems the gums are particularly sensitive to these things. Now tell me, would you have the strength to endure such a diabolical transformation?"

Cal searched for the right answer. "Probably not."

"What is your name, crewman?" the Lizard King asked, grinning wide, almost from ear to ear.

"Caladon Heit."

"It is a regret that our time together must be so short, Caladon Heit. But your planet needs you! Apparently," he said, almost incredulous. "Although no one can trespass through my domain without paying a price."

He leaned back on his throne. The crew of *Fidelity* looked at each other in uncertainty.

"I permit you to offer another in your place. A tithe, to show your respect to me. Bring me a starship and its crew as payment, at least as many as are aboard your own vessel, and you shall be forgiven. Fail me in this, and you and your own vessel will be forfeit. I will dispatch my reavers to find you and claim you, and they will be inescapable. Your rustic ship can never hide from me again." He shook his head in mock condolence. "This is my decree!" he boomed suddenly.

Cal nearly fell backward.

"A life for a life. A ship for a ship. A debt has begun, and your time will be short. I will anticipate the fruit of your efforts. Don't disappoint me." The Lizard King gestured to the wider court around him. "Send these fools on their way."

*

"It wounds the pride a little, doesn't it? To not even be considered worthy of robbing," Cal said.

He and the rest of the crew were all back on the bridge of *Fidelity* without any of the pirates. Their ship was still inside the asteroid base, but they'd been told they were free to launch away.

"Shut up, Cal," Major Rosco said. "You've said more than enough about this mission so far."

Around them, technicians and bridge crew rushed to ready *Fidelity* for launch as quickly as possible. Bright glowing screens flashed back to life, and a whining noise occasionally emanated from deeper in the ship as the reactor powered up from hibernation.

"I got us out of there, didn't I?" Cal protested.

"Nothing about this mission is a joke," Rosco said.

"I don't recall making any jokes," Cal muttered to himself.

"Don't you have work to do?"

"I am working," Cal said, pointing at his console at the desk in front of him. "What are you meant to be doing?"

"I provide security on the bridge, as well as ongoing tactical analysis," Rosco said.

"Well, you've nailed it so far."

"You jumped us into this star system in the first place!" Rosco said in disbelief.

"That was Yendos." Cal looked around the bridge again, but Yendos was nowhere to be seen.

"All hands prepare for immediate launch," Captain Haran told the entire ship.

The iron portcullis had withdrawn from the entrance to the asteroid's docking bay. The holes melted by the boarding tube had been patched. The last clamps and cables binding *Fidelity* to the asteroid were disconnected. They received a clear-to-launch signal from the pirates.

"Connect me to the pilot," Leda said.

A moment of awkward silence passed throughout the bridge. Everyone waited to see what would happen.

Leda looked around and saw everyone watching her. "I need to establish a new baseline peak for our reactor if we want to fast burn out of here, but all our calibrated metrics are gone after our reactor was sitting idle for so long. I can't determine the rate at which the thruster's drawing energy unless I know exactly what maneuvers the pilot's trying to do." Leda explained it like it was obvious. "You don't want us to blow the radiation valves on the ignition system."

Captain Haran looked displeased. "Connect Engineer Palchek to the pilot's cockpit," she said.

Cal smiled. The pilot's secret identity was over.

The bridge crew cheered as the ship left the asteroid mouth and they returned to open space.

Chapter 12

Captain Haran felt a sense of pride as *Fidelity* arrived at the Grand Highway of Thelmia. She'd expected the ship to reach its target here, but it was a significant achievement nonetheless. The Grand Highway was busy. More starships were active here than had even been present in the Paxis system. The average size class of the vessels moving through the Highway was larger than anything they'd seen before. A majority were civilian, unarmed freighters and tankers like theirs supposedly was, traveling on business through a major artery across the galaxy. The Highway felt orderly, a place of security, at last. A handful of imposing and well-armed warships were positioned along the route, but they were stationary.

With their magnetic dampening unit fully functioning, *Fidelity* would pass among all the other vessels as just another freighter unless they were scanned at a very close range.

The jump out of this system was critical to the timeline of their journey. No other route would get them to the Ruarken Senate with a realistic chance of protecting Vale Reach, Captain Haran knew. The Highway was always the critical bottleneck they were heading for. According to estimates, they'd barely avoided the effects of time debt so far. More than any other jump, the far end of the Highway would take them to truly distant regions. The star system around them had two suns and many planets, but despite a network of orbital docks around several planets, the planets were judged to be of minimal value. The long-distance transit points were all that mattered.

Captain Haran directed *Fidelity* to approach the main flow of traffic and enter a shipping lane. Even in a system as dense as the Highway, starships were typically still separated from each other by many thousands of kilometers. At that distance, every detail could be clearly seen visually. *Fidelity* slotted into place amidst a matrix of vessels leading toward the far transit point. The crew seemed to collectively breathe a sigh of relief. Haran was pleased. They'd earned their moment of peace.

Only a short time later, an alarm sounded on the bridge, shattering the calm. Haran saw one of the officers had registered a hostile ship.

"The Enforcer ship has arrived through the transit point behind us!" Leda said. "It's the same vessel as before. This is our fourth encounter with them," she confirmed.

"Are they scanning us?" Captain Haran asked.

"That's confirmed," Cal said. "They've accelerated! They've changed heading to directly intercept us."

"We're receiving a message from them," Leda said.

"Play it." Haran turned to Advocate Fargas. "Ready to translate?"

"Let's do it," Fargas said to her as Councilor Theeran came to stand by her captain's chair.

The main screen was filled with the image of another ship's bridge. Like their own ship, the bridge they saw was of a rotating cylindrical design, so the other ship's crew were sitting at every angle as they looked into whatever camera had recorded the message.

The Enforcer ship's bridge was dark but not totally unlike *Fidelity*'s. The upside-down faces uncomfortably reminded Haran of what she'd seen in the Lizard King's court. It occurred to her that they themselves would look the same to an outside observer. The Enforcer bridge's surfaces were raw, unpainted metal but rounded and smooth. A series of railings like ladders were mounted onto all the walls. Men were strapped into chairs, facing computer consoles, with hard, angry stares on their faces. Captain Haran was struck by how ethnically homogeneous they looked, compared to the other crews they'd seen so far. That, too, mirrored their own ship.

The Enforcer captain was seated on a raised command chair, alone at the center of the ship. He barked a series of orders directly into the recording.

"It's their usual routine," Fargas said. "'Shut down engines, prepare for inspection.'"

"Why are they coming after us?" Captain Haran asked.

"Well, these aren't really the kind of people concerned with asking why," Fargas said. "They believe in taking action. Once they've decided to inspect us, they must carry it out. That's how they establish authority, even within the crew of their own ship. Their captain wouldn't be respected if he didn't follow through on everything. A power structure like that can't allow even the slightest challenge to stand. The Enforcers probably decided to board us four star systems back when they first saw us. If they fail at it now, their authority as Enforcers would disappear. It's a matter of principle for these guys. Duty, I guess they would call it."

"So absolutely no chance they could be bribed or distracted?" Councilor Theeran asked.

Fargas shook his head. "Definitely not. Once the Enforcers have decided something, they will never stop coming for you till it's done. Which, in our case, is going to mean a thorough audit of our interior, at minimum."

"What are the consequences if we refuse?" Theeran asked.

"Their mood at present seems irritable," Fargas said. "They don't appreciate having to come all the way here to get us."

Captain Haran tapped her fingers on the armrest of her chair for a few moments. As ever, *Fidelity* being boarded by a proxy for the Universal Legion was not an option. The Enforcer ship was already close, so they had very limited means of escape. Yet there were no alternatives. Haran nodded to herself as she realized the certainty of their situation. Her fists slowly clenched. She turned to Councilor Theeran. "It may be time to escalate things. We knew this moment would come. Seeking your permission to engage our contingency evasion plan."

"We have no choice," Theeran agreed. "If they get one look at our computers, they'll discover who we are immediately." He took a breath and nodded. "So let's do it."

Haran turned to look back at the rest of the bridge. "Engage Plan Theta, escape and evasion protocol."

*

All systems aboard *Fidelity* powered up to their maximum levels. The forces on the crew were intense. Captain Haran read every graph on her personal screen. The reactor reached the highest rate of burn recorded so far. The overheated power was explosively vented out through their thrusters to add to the acceleration. The atmospheric canopy engaged across the front of the ship in anticipation of any immersion or collision. Dozens of gas-powered turning engines arranged in rows on the *Fidelity*'s exterior raised themselves to their optimum temperature, and the functionality of each unit was tested with short bursts. Haran checked the synthesized fuel from Allumia was loaded, then she turned her attention to the engine room. Extra layers of shielding were closing around the reactor to contain any gamma spikes and thermal flashes that could emit from the ship's fiery core. The engineers that labored in its shadow were skillfully raising its energy output up to a raging torrent. The full power of the reactor was awakened, ready for her to command from the bridge.

"Pilot, you have full control to bring us out of the traffic lanes. Get us down into Planet Fifteen, Sigma Quadrant," Captain Haran said. "Begin the descent to the atmosphere now."

The turning engines brought *Fidelity* out of position in a corkscrew dive. They traveled with a chaotically enlarging spiral path, as unpredictable as possible.

"Keep our emissions low," Haran said. "Make us hard to find."

Planet Fifteen, Sigma Quadrant was near, large in their viewing screens. *Fidelity* headed straight into its dark side. Behind them, they detected the Enforcer ship in close pursuit.

"The Enforcer ship is powering up its gamma lasers," Leda reported. 'They'll open fire soon. Any moment."

That was the point Captain Haran had dreaded and prepared for more than anything else since *Fidelity* had first launched.

"Shut down everything except our engines. Keep us moving randomly. Brace for impact!" Captain Haran said.

The Enforcer ship opened fire, releasing a pulse of high-power energy from each of its laser cannons. The weapons emitted a flicker of searing thermal radiation that lasted several seconds. If *Fidelity*'s position had been known, the Enforcers could've concentrated their lasers to a narrow point that would slice through *Fidelity*'s hull with ease. A shield generator would've been able to protect them, but that was far beyond the technology of Vale Reach. Haran ensured that *Fidelity* had hidden itself in the time before the attack, by obscuring their signal and scrambling their position. A thinly focused beam stood almost no chance of hitting them in empty space. Instead, the Enforcers had no choice but to calibrate their weapons to a wide burn, radiating the energy through a wide region of space as an unfocused spread. *Fidelity* instantaneously took damage. One whole side of the hull heated up like a sunburn. Sparks erupted as pipes burst and cables melted within the ship's hull. Several small compartments of the ship began to uncontrollably decompress as air leaked out through cracks. Haran felt the damage as almost physical pain as she watched the data. Each of the breached areas sealed with no loss of crew reported. After just three seconds, the energy bombardment ceased as the Enforcer ship readied its capacitors to strike again. Haran breathed in relief. They'd survived the first strike. There'd been no certainty that *Fidelity* could withstand any major laser hit.

"Get us down into Planet Fifteen now," Captain Haran said. "Get us in the atmosphere immediately."

The ship lurched from side to side as it made sharp, random movements. All the crew held on tight. Some crew members prayed. While Marraz directed the ship with all his expertise and determination, they could only wait as the Enforcer's ship recharged its capacitors. Agonizing minutes passed. The Enforcer ship opened fire again.

Fidelity didn't shake or rock as it was hit by the widespread gamma rays. Instead, the metal of the hull creaked and popped as it became heated far beyond its tolerances. The noise echoed through the interior as *Fidelity* stretched and bent. Wall panels bulged inward and outward. Haran registered more splits and breaches, each accompanied by a minor explosion of atmospheric gases. Wiring went dead, like the numb nerves of a body, as they melted to the point of disintegration. Haran ordered crew members stationed near the hull to retreat back from their stations and shelter behind thick bulkhead doorways. After another three seconds, the damage was done.

"Damage report!" Captain Haran ordered.

For a few frantic, intense moments, the bridge crew urgently analyzed the extent of the system failures. Most internal sensors were overwhelmed with errors and showed garbled nonsense, as instruments around the ship registered their maximum values or transmitted white noise. As she watched the hardware cool, Haran felt relief as many of the ship's systems returned to reporting normal levels again.

"Another set of minor hull breaches—no crew lost," Leda reported. "We have some void-suited repair teams that can go in and plug the gaps with sealant foam so we can repressurize the compartments."

"Not until we're out of the line of fire," Haran said.

"Around a quarter of the maneuvering engines are offline," another officer reported. "Many of the external sensor probes on one side have burned out."

"Elements of Planet Fifteen's atmosphere are around us now," Cal said. "We're getting deeper down into the layers. We should be mostly concealed before they can fire at us again."

"Unless they fire at reduced charge for some immediate damage," Leda said.

"Report to me on the path of the Enforcer ship," Haran said.

"They show all signs of following us," Leda said. "They're coming right down into the atmosphere behind us."

That was as Captain Haran expected.

The skies were red and orange over Planet Fifteen. Like all worlds, it had an official name, perhaps multiple, but that didn't matter. Thick storms threw their ship from side to side. They were now fully inside the planet's atmosphere, the front deflector driving a path through the gloom. At the speed they were traveling, each cloud hit them with enough momentum to rattle the whole ship. The lower they descended, the more opaque the skies became above them and the more protected they were from laser damage. Occasionally, *Fidelity* reached a pocket of empty air in the clouds, and the screens showed a view toward the horizon that stretched for thousands of miles across the gas giant.

"Reduce the main thruster to low power. Cool the temperature," Captain Haran said. "We can use the air friction on the deflector to control our path." *Fidelity* could minimize its energy output to aid their disappearance among the clouds.

"The Enforcers aren't far away," Cal reported. "They aren't hiding their signals much. I detected a significant heat signature as they entered the cloud level. They're pushing through the atmospheric burn at a huge temperature, a much faster velocity than we can manage."

A starship could travel through vacuum far faster than through any kind of air, Haran knew. Any spaceship descending into gas clouds would experience significant deceleration and immense heat friction. *Fidelity* was limited in the speed they could push through the thick atmosphere, or else they would break apart from extreme turbulence. The Enforcers' ship, with its armored front prow and energy shields, could tolerate far higher entry heat and could plunge deeper and faster through the murky gases of the planet than *Fidelity*.

"The Enforcers may have actually overtaken us by now," Cal said. "We can't tell if they're ahead of us or behind."

If *Fidelity* entered into an empty patch of clouds and the Enforcers were waiting for them, their ship could be hit by a close-range laser strike. That would mean death for them all.

"We need something more," Captain Haran said. "We need a powerful storm. A big one."

Haran brought up a series of map locations on screen. The only data they had about their environment was from simple visual analysis as they passed between the ochre clouds.

"Here, bring us into this." She directed them toward a massive turbulent vortex towering over the planet.

Fidelity swerved, and everyone aboard was thrown to one side as it changed direction. The ship maneuvered completely differently inside an atmosphere. Far steeper turning angles could be achieved using the air resistance, but breaking apart spectacularly was an ever-present danger. The entire structure of the ship was facing stress forces far higher than it had been designed to handle. If the ship turned too sharply and too fast, the wind forces would shear through the metal.

As they approached the vast storm, the bridge screens showed the face of the vortex, the external wall of the hurricane beyond which chaos awaited. The twisting pillar of vapor rose over the world like the unlimited wrath of god and tumbled down into the bottomless depths below.

"Report on the Enforcers' ship," Captain Haran said.

"It's close," Cal said.

Fidelity risked annihilation if they hesitated to take cover.

"Take us inside," Captain Haran said. "We'll be impossible to find. Brace for turbulence."

The screens grew dark as they passed into the vortex.

Everyone aboard was violently shaken. The forces were frenzied, lurching them in a different direction each fraction of a second. The crew fought to keep a tight grip on their surroundings. All crew had strapped into their seats as per Haran's orders. She tightened the belts across herself as far as they could go. The disruption caused by the ship's juddering was terrifying, putting a strain on their nerves and senses. The crew risked suffering shaken-brain injuries if they endured too much of the convulsing motion. Haran decided the risks were acceptable. She forced herself to overcome her sense of nausea. After the months spent aboard a rotating ship, her body had managed to adjust to all manner of continuous unnatural gravitational effects.

The view outside from every external camera was black. No light entered the storm clouds. The crew all clung on tightly and waited, enduring the elements and praying for time to pass. The engineers in the reactor room were fighting to keep the reactor stable and contained. The pilot in the cockpit had direct control of the ship's orientation as he tried to ride them through the currents. The ship's survival rested in their hands. The thruster roared, and the front engines whined as they fought to hold the ship in a steady position. The energy levels from the reactor trembled at their peak as the propulsion system demanded sudden spikes of unpredictable high power.

Haran considered what their next move should be, hoping the Enforcer ship, whether it had entered the vortex with them or remained somewhere outside, had lost all trace of them. If they were lucky, it would leave the area, hunting for some other sign of their trail. No indicator showed that the Enforcers had entered the titanic hurricane. Haran wondered whether what *Fidelity* had done would be considered a suicidal action for a Palladian freighter, as well as how the Enforcer ship had even found them. The Enforcers must have been searching in each system they entered. Potentially, they could have set up an observation post on the Highway to warn them of *Fidelity*'s arrival. Despite the magnetic dampening unit, the Enforcer ship could still recognize them through visual means as they'd had plenty of time to study *Fidelity*'s structure in the first system they'd met. *Fidelity* had small idiosyncrasies in the design that couldn't be hidden. Visual identification techniques would fail over a long enough distance, though. *Fidelity* had to get far away from its pursuer then successfully shelter among similar freighters. That was possible. If it wasn't, they would have to somehow make it possible. They couldn't relent until either they escaped or were destroyed.

The skies cleared around one of *Fidelity*'s viewing windows. They had reached a wide-open space at the core of the vortex. Captain Haran looked downward and saw through the eye of the storm, deep into the planet, a tunnel heading straight to oblivion. A gas giant had literally no ground. Any object would fall infinitely till the gases formed a scalding ocean. If *Fidelity* tumbled into this vortex, their melted bones would eternally writhe in a crushing limbo for endless billions of years. The ship would plummet to its doom if any of its engines failed. She looked back at her computer screen. Nearly every reading on the reactor's performance had been pushed into the red.

She opened a video link to the engine room. "Engine room, report on your status."

They were all visibly struggling to hold on and stay in position as they were shaken by the ship's tumbling motion. Not all the engineers had the security of remaining in their seats. The room around them was lit by bright waves of blue energy that flashed electric white as the reactor flared. Five engineers, including the chief, were clinging to the outside of its shield casing at the center of the room, where gravity was weak. They were replacing burned-out components, she realized, changing wiring and bypassing dead pieces in the control system. Other members of the engineering crew were seated at their stations, reading data and issuing commands to the reactor through their consoles. Maintaining the ship's current position against the sucking forces of the storm demanded the reactor be sustained at the highest intensity they could manage. The engineers were doing everything in their power to keep the core fully operational as pieces of the system began to fail, but Captain Haran could clearly see they were burning through material. It was untenable. The reactor's containment was being held together by nothing more than hasty repairs and human willpower.

"All crew, prepare to change course." She switched her transmission to speak with just the bridge. "We make a launch for the blue moon here." Captain Haran brought up its image on screen. "It's aligned in a path ahead of us. We come up out of the vortex fast. The reactor is already running hot—we can vent out the whole plasma load for a speed boost. When we reach the blue moon, we can use its natural gravity to bring us around in a low pass orbit close over the moon's surface. If we get our power levels back down to a dormant state in the far side of the moon's shadow, there's no way the Enforcers can continue to track our signal. They'll have to search for us manually. It'll take them a long time. It might not even be possible." Haran instructed the bridge crew. "We'll be exposed to laser fire for forty seconds as we get there. I can't guarantee your safety. Prepare yourselves."

*

Fidelity emerged from the clouds, rocketing up toward space. The raging orange vortex shrank away beneath them, as did the whole surface of the planet. Less than ten seconds later, the Enforcer ship burst through the clouds behind them and opened fire.

Fidelity had selected a nearly direct path to reach the moon as quickly as possible, and so the Enforcers' ship attacked with a more focused beam.

The gamma beam swept through the void, slashing out at *Fidelity*. It missed their ship, cutting through empty space. The crew released a breath of relief. Eight seconds passed before the Enforcers' ship fired again. The second swipe of the beam struck their hull, burning a gash two decks deep across the surface of *Fidelity*, leaving a glowing orange line where it cut into the ship as it rotated. Anyone caught in its path was disintegrated. Despite the damage, *Fidelity's* thruster power remained undiminished. The ship continued at maximum acceleration as the Enforcers charged their gamma lasers once more. With the split in its side, *Fidelity* was ejecting a trail of hot matter in its wake, droplets of molten metal and plumes of scorched fiber and burnt black ash. The third laser strike hit them directly. It carved along one side of the ship, detaching a large piece of the exterior and depressurizing four decks. *Fidelity* kept itself aimed at the blue moon and reduced its thrusters momentarily. The Enforcer ship charged its capacitors for a fourth strike, likely narrowing their weapon to its most concentrated setting as *Fidelity*'s leaking damage revealed its position. The instant before the weapons discharged, *Fidelity* blasted its thrusters for one final chaotic maximum burn and hurled itself into an uncontrolled descent toward the moon. The Enforcers' energy beam lashed out but found nothing but vacuum. *Fidelity* shut off all power entirely. The moon's gravity carried *Fidelity* in a natural arc across its rocky blue surface and out of line of sight from their attacker. The curvature of the moon's hard terrestrial body shielded them from the laser weapons of the Enforcer ship. Captain Haran watched the signals of the Enforcer ship fade as they sheltered behind the moon. Even the scanning systems of an advanced warship would have difficulty detecting their emissions directly through an object of such density. *Fidelity* had entered the gravity well first, but the Enforcer ship would likely still be close behind them. As fast as it was able, the Enforcer ship would sweep over the moon and search the far side for them.

"All hands begin emergency repair procedure," Captain Haran ordered. "Major Rosco, begin a search for any survivors in the breached decks."

*

Rosco hurried down the corridor of *Fidelity* wearing a space suit, the dome helmet already in place over his head. Gravity had returned to normal aboard the ship now, and the disruptive forces from their evasive maneuvers were gone. At the end of the corridor, a heavy metal door had closed where no door had been before.

"I'm at the breach," Rosco reported to the bridge.

He walked up to the door, which had a metal panel that could move like a shutter. He moved it aside to reveal a transparent window section and peered through. The other side was dark. The ship had been built with small battery-powered lamps in the walls that activated if the main power was cut. Some of those were operational on the other side, and they emitted weak electric light in the space beyond the emergency bulkhead door. Rosco could see no movement at all. He took a short length of metal cable attached to his space suit and secured it to a nearby wall. Then he shut a door farther behind him in the corridor and prepared to depressurize the area where he was standing. The bulkhead door opened, and for a few seconds, he felt the air being sucked out all around him. He held on tightly to the metal cable securing him and stayed on his feet. Then he was in the silent vacuum, with the dark room open ahead of him. He stepped over the threshold into the ruptured decks.

The area had been cut open by a gamma laser. Rosco looked at the perfectly straight line melted through the floor. It was four inches wide, and he saw black space outside through the gap, with stars twinkling brightly. The cut stretched away out of sight, passing through doorways and under a wall. Around it, the metal had been warped into a shape of rippling water by the laser's heat but was frozen solid once again to form a razor-sharp edge. He flipped on the light of his helmet to look around the room. Rosco saw human remains, hands and parts of boots or pieces of scalp with the flesh melted black. Dark scorch marks also covered all the walls. As soon as the laser had breached the compartment, temperatures skyrocketed. Nothing could have survived or would be salvageable.

"I've arrived at the breached decks. Everything has been destroyed by the heat. Continuing the search for other survivors," Rosco said.

"Negative," came the reply. "There's no time. You're needed back on the bridge. Confirm it's safe for repair teams to enter. Then return to your station."

Rosco sighed. "It's stable to come patch up." He flicked off his flashlight.

*

"I see signals from the Enforcer ship. It's starting to come round the horizon," Cal said. "There're only reflections from the clouds so far, but they could enter this area soon."

Fidelity had stayed hidden for several hours, but the arrival of the Enforcer ship once again was exactly what they'd been desperate to avoid.

"What are the chances that they can locate us here?" Captain Haran asked.

"The cloud cover here isn't what we hoped. We're probably visible if they get within about three hundred kilometers," Leda said.

Captain Haran thought about that for a moment. "That's not good enough. We need a plan to get out of here. Start warming up the engines, but keep the heat contained inside."

"We're building up harmful isotopes in the reactor if we go down that path," Leda said. "We'll need to vent some very dangerous radiation soon."

"Tell the engineers to be prepared for it," Haran said. "We need an escape plan to successfully get away from this position. Put me through to the pilot."

Fidelity was equipped with a number of decoy-signal buoys on board, ready to launch in situations such as the one they currently faced. If the Enforcers followed the buoy and left the area, even momentarily, *Fidelity* could dash away at full speed, once again putting the entire moon between themselves and their pursuers. If *Fidelity* could get near the Highway before the Enforcers discovered the deception, the Enforcers would have to identify them again amid the noise of signals coming from the traffic, and *Fidelity* could make an exit from the system before they were caught.

"Pilot, are you ready to execute the launch from the moon back toward the Highway and the transit points?" Captain Haran asked.

Marraz's voice came over the intercom. "I'm ready. Let's give it everything."

"Release the decoy," she ordered.

"I register a change in direction by the Enforcer ship," Cal reported.

They were following it. "Pilot, get us low and fast around the moon. Engines quiet till we're around the horizon, then bring us up to maximum and do a steep-angle turn once we're back at the moon's far side."

"Acknowledged," Marraz said.

Fidelity crept away from where it had launched the decoy, running the reactor at a minimal power level. The reflections of the Enforcer ship from the clouds grew fainter and disappeared again.

"Keep us low," Captain Haran said.

If the Enforcer ship was pursuing the decoy as hoped, a quarter of the moon's circumference would soon be between them.

"Prepare for a high-power launch maneuver," Captain Haran said.

Everyone once again clung on to something stable or tightened their chair harness.

"On my mark," Captain Haran said, "spike power to the engines for a maximum burn of ten seconds. Launch us out to space, up toward the Highway. I want explosive power. Then a full shutdown on all emissions to hide us."

"Systems report the reactor is ready," Leda said. "The engine room's contained the level of toxic isotopes."

"Now!" Captain Haran said.

Fidelity's engines ignited. More fuel poured into the reactor. Nuclear fire flowed out from the thruster with a fierce roar. The ship accelerated with the maximum force it was capable of.

"Use the air pressure to give us the steepest launch angle," Captain Haran said.

Inside his cockpit, Marraz gripped the primary control stick and yanked it upward.

The engines of *Fidelity* threw the ship up away from the moon. Part of the front atmospheric shield broke away, weakened by the Enforcers' laser damage. Inside the ship, bent metal support beams creaked and folded. Structural failures spread across the ship, cascading out from one another until the damaged side of *Fidelity* crumpled and collapsed inward. Maneuvering engines failed or were ripped out of position. *Fidelity* wildly spun end over end, more pieces of exterior being shredded and torn away by wind forces as they tumbled wildly through the atmosphere, inflicting even more damage. Apocalyptic screeching and wailing noises filled the ship as walls and decks stretched and broke apart. The main thruster sputtered and died, and they rapidly lost velocity. They were drifting without control, high in the moon's upper orbit.

Chapter 13

The ship had no gravity. Leda was floating weightlessly as was everyone else aboard. The bridge was totally lightless, darker than it ever had been. For a few seconds, everyone was dazed from the shock of the ship's structural failure.

"What's happened to our power?" Captain Haran asked.

The crew were quiet as they attempted to get any information from their computer systems. Loose objects drifted in the air although the bridge crew remained held in their seats. Emergency batteries activated to provide some very limited power for the computers to function.

"One of the science labs has collapsed," Cal said. "It's shorted out all our internal circuitry. Several of our dynamic conduit relays exploded."

"Get the power back to the bridge immediately," Captain Haran told the crew.

"The reactor won't restart," Leda said. "The ignition systems have overheated, and the safety locks have engaged. The reactor's gone into a protective shutdown until it cools." Leda momentarily ground her teeth in frustration. "It's going to take a while for engineering to restart it. Most of their instruments have burnt out."

"Can we restart our artificial gravity?" Captain Haran asked.

Leda studied the screen closely. "There's a very small number of working rotational engines, but I have access to them. I set them to stabilize us and restore gravity. It's starting now, but it could take a while."

They drifted, silent and lightless, in a wide cloud of their own debris. Leda studied the reactor's status thoroughly, but from her position on the bridge, she could do little to influence it. The external structural damage had been terrible too. The ship must have lost more crew. Even if they regained power, the ship was crippled.

Two loud noises shook the vessel, one after the other.

"We've been hit," Cal reported. "Some kind of hard impact. Maybe it's a rail gun strike."

"A direct rail gun strike could've ripped us apart." Major Rosco addressed the ship's communications line. "Have we sustained any fresh hull breaches? All crew, report."

Leda found something on *Fidelity*'s camera network. "Major! I've received something." Rosco floated over to her position, where she showed him an image one of the crew had sent to the bridge. An object several meters wide and with long spikes filled a compartment. It had pierced deep through several layers of walls and flooring. Despite the object having burst in from the outside, the impact site was still mostly pressurized, as the compacted metal formed a tight seal.

"Shit," Rosco muttered. "It's a harpoon, sir," he called to Captain Haran. "Check for a second one," he told Leda.

As he'd predicted, she found the site of another harpoon strike. "They're at either end of the ship."

"I'm doing a visual search," Cal said. "Most of the optical scopes on the surface have been knocked out. I've found one in good condition." He was quiet for a second. "There they are. The Enforcer ship is here."

The main screen on the bridge came to life on its lowest power setting. Its weak light dimly illuminated the bridge.

Cal transferred the image from the optical scope to the main screen, and the bridge gazed at the sight of the opposing vessel. Its front cone was flat and angular, made of smooth armored metal. Behind that was a thick trunk with a radius many times wider than *Fidelity,* along with four cannons that reached out from different directions to target them. Leda manually directed scanning tools at the vessel to study it further.

"They're charging their laser capacitors to full power," she reported. "The weapons have focused their arrays directly at our position."

Captain Haran was quiet for a moment. "We're at their mercy. But they're waiting. They could have blasted us apart already. They haven't yet, so let's see what they want."

The Enforcer ship came close to *Fidelity,* maneuvering to within fifty meters. Leda watched through her console screens as a dozen angled thrusters across its surface quickly moved the ship to be end to end with their own vessel. She estimated the Enforcer ship was at least five times the size of *Fidelity*.

Boarding tubes snaked out from the front of the Enforcer ship and reached across space to bite into the front end of their ship.

"Here we go again," Cal said.

"At least they've attached to our boarding ports this time." Leda looked closer at her screen as a distant explosion was heard inside. "Never mind. They've just blasted apart the boarding ports without opening them." She gritted her teeth again in anger and frustration.

"Two voidcraft have launched from their hangar bay," Cal said, fear in his voice. "They're reached our own hangar bay already. Should… should we open the bay doors for them?"

Yet another explosion echoed through the ship. She wondered how much more damage their ship could sustain.

"Missile strike," Leda said. "They've hit us with some kind of explosive rocket."

"They've destroyed the hangar bay doors," an officer reported. "Their voidcraft are already inside. Prepare for—" Several warning alarms sounded in the bridge. "Prepare for hostile entry of the hangar bay."

Leda got no response from the hangar bay decks. All contact had been lost. Her apprehension became unbearable. She felt like a trapped animal.

"The engineering levels are compromised," Captain Haran said. "They're coming for the bridge. Likely a specialized boarding team. Prepare for their arrival, but leave the internal doors open," she said. "Let's try not to get more of our ship blown up."

In under a minute, the Enforcers squad arrived on the bridge. By then, a noticeable level of gravity had returned to the ship. Each of the Enforcers carried a large rifle and wore matte-black armor over their whole bodies, atop a black undersuit. Only their faces were uncovered. The angry snarls were much as they'd looked in the video message sent, wide-eyed and frozen in stern fury.

The Enforcers spread slowly and mistrustfully through the bridge, their weapons aimed at all the *Fidelity* crew. One man aimed the barrel of his weapon directly at Leda, bringing it close to her face, and she felt a dizzying rush of adrenaline.

She dared to look down at her console. A squad of at least twenty Enforcers had arrived through the launch bay. Even then, additional Enforcer troops were pouring in through the boarding tubes to occupy all the corridors of the *Fidelity*.

The Enforcers moved to take positions all around the ship, keeping their guns pointed at any crew they found. The bridge crew tried to remain calm and impassive, awaiting some next course of action.

Leda watched as one Enforcer headed straight toward Captain Haran, moving more purposely and faster than the others. Without hesitating, the Enforcer drew a metal baton from his uniform and hit Captain Haran across the head with it. The sound of the crack echoed, and the whole bridge crew gasped in shock as she fell to the ground. The Enforcer hit her in the head several more times until she was completely still. Leda felt she might vomit.

Then she looked up and saw someone new standing in the doorway to the bridge. It was a member of the pirate gang. No one else had seen this person yet. Bright electric-blue-and-orange patterns swirled across her outfit, and she carried a pair of gleaming silver daggers. Leda saw hatchways and panels start loosening around the bridge. Leda froze in shock. Like spiders unfolding from a nest, pirates burst out from hidden compartments and floor plates around the bridge, unwinding their gangly limbs as they erupted free. From every direction, brightly colored warriors leapt from the spaces between decks. The pirate leader at the bridge entrance threw her dagger just as the Enforcer squad leader turned to look in her direction. The blade hit him in the neck, sending him crashing to the ground.

The entire room seemed to explode as the Enforcer squad opened fire on the pirates.

Leda dropped to the floor and tried to crawl under her console. Dark-gray smoke filled the bridge, along with the seemingly endless detonations of hand grenades. Peering out through the haze, she saw jets of orange sparks explode out as the bridge was torn up. Feet and bodies were rolling around, men and women locked in hand-to-hand combat for their lives—pirates, Enforcers, and bridge crew alike. They were tangled in a storm of gunfire, humans, and shrapnel. The Enforcers were forming a circle in the center of the room, their guns blasting, but the pirates were already among them and cutting them down. More Enforcers piled in against the pirates, wielding their own knives and short pistols, trying to overwhelm their enemies with superior numbers. Cal saw two pirates dragged down by multiple Enforcers and riddled with bullets at point-blank range. The pirate leader cut through the Enforcers at an ever-faster rate. The number of Enforcers was rapidly diminishing, she realized.

Leda watched as Cal rose from cover and dashed away from the bridge, running through the smoke and over the bodies. She got up and ran after him. She immediately crashed into someone in a *Fidelity* security uniform as they stumbled backward. It was Major Rosco. He'd taken a gun from one of the Enforcers.

"Leda, get out of here!" he shouted at her.

She scrambled out the doorway to the bridge and sprinted down the corridor. As she ran, she saw an Enforcement officer standing at a doorway, his weapon aimed at her. Then a pirate appeared from behind him and tackled the Enforcer to the ground. A jet of bright blood sprayed out as the pirate cut the Enforcer's throat. The fighting was happening everywhere in the ship, she realized, not just on the bridge. Leda accelerated and tumbled around a corner. She took cover in an alcove. Cal was sheltering in the corner next to hers. He looked back out at her but didn't say anything. They needed to get farther away from the carnage in the bridge. As she prepared to get up and run again, she heard an angry alarm that was coming from her datapad. The sound was something she'd only heard in training simulations, but it registered through her fear. A criticality event had occurred in one of the reactor's fuel units. Through some malfunction, a heavy isotope cell in the reactor was heating up inexorably. If they couldn't eject it quickly, the ship would be irreparably damaged, and the whole vessel would ultimately be destroyed. She ducked low as a grenade exploded nearby. No one in the engine room had done anything to resolve the situation and remove the cell. Leda had to assume the engineering decks were disabled by the fighting. The cameras on the bridge had shown Enforcer squads overtake that area.

Someone ran up to her position. It was Rosco, she was desperately relieved to see. "Get to one of the storerooms for shelter," he told her, grabbing her arm.

"No, wait. I have to stabilize the reactor," she urgently told him.

"Are you serious?" Rosco asked in disbelief.

"Yes, absolutely." She went to show him the datapad, but he waved it away. "Cal, we need you!" she yelled over at him.

After a moment of hesitation, Cal came over to her. "What the hell? What's happening?" he demanded.

"There's been a criticality event in one of the fuel cells," she told him.

"Oh fuck!" he yelled, almost furious as the implications set in. "Now? God damn it."

"Listen to me," she told Cal. Their internal radio system was offline, so she had to be very specific. "Two things need to happen. You are going to do one of these things, and I am going to do the other, understand? I go into the reactor control room and manually eject the corrupted cell out into space. But the consoles are likely all blown out. You have to get to a server room and restart the mainframe network. Unplug everything if you have to. That'll give me one minute where I can directly operate the reactor, bypassing all the consoles."

Cal exhaled, wide-eyed and pupils dilated with fear. "It's going to be tough."

"You have to make it," Leda said. "There's no other way. No one else is active in the reactor room right now. No one's going to fix it if we don't."

Cal nodded. "We can't ignore this, can we? There's no other way."

Gunshots were still very loud and nearby.

"I can't go with both of you." Rosco looked distressed, as though guilty. "I'm going with Leda. I'm sorry, Cal. Don't let yourself get hurt. Don't hesitate to hide or kill if you need to. I'll see you on the other side." He put a hand on Cal's back.

Cal patted him back in response. "I can do this. We have to make this work, together," Cal said.

"Let's go!" Rosco said.

*

Cal ran through a junction and turned another corner. Two more pirates in fluorescent outfits were hacking apart a group of Enforcers. *Fidelity* crewmen were dead on the floor, too, cut through by those same blades. The two pirates looked up to face him, their enemies dead. Cal backed away but found himself against a locked door. He watched in horror as the pirates came toward him. A large doorway opened to the side of them, and a dozen Enforcers came through with their guns ready. The pirates burst apart, shredded in a hail of bullets. Cal remembered the correct code for the door behind him and opened it using a control panel. He squeezed through just as the Enforcers began to shoot at him, hiding on the far side of the door frame as he waited for the door to close again. He heard the Enforcers against the door, but it was locked shut. Cal looked around. Other science officers were in the room with him, sheltering behind equipment, a small group of four. He'd entered one of the undamaged lab facilities.

"We have to shut down everything in the server room," Cal told them. He was breathless, almost unable to speak. "The reactor's in a criticality event. We need to manually eject the fuel rods."

They all nodded.

"It's vital. The ship is wrecked otherwise."

A loud detonation nearby rattled the room. The Enforcers were trying to breach the door Cal had entered through, using explosives.

"How can we get out of here?" he asked in desperation.

One of the science officers was already moving. "We can exit out the back. There's a hatch that leads to a maintenance tunnel, but the area outside that is probably compromised."

"Hurry," Cal said.

*

Rosco heard the gunfire and explosions throughout every part of the ship as he ran behind Leda. He couldn't imagine the number of possible casualties among the crew. He'd lost count of how many grenades he'd heard. The sounds of fighting and screaming came from all around. Rosco and Leda arrived at the junction leading to the engine room and saw the door to the engine room was open. Inside, a tall figure wearing a blood-red jumpsuit and a skull mask turned and saw them. At his feet were a mountain of dead Enforcers. No one else was left alive in the reactor room.

Leda stopped and looked at Rosco in uncertainty. Rosco gestured for her to get behind him. The pirate in the red suit was coming toward the doorway.

"We need to eject one of the fuel rods," Leda shouted at him, "or else there's going to be a deadly radiation burst!"

The pirate put both hands on his hips. "This is not my ship," he said through his mask. "What do I care if it melts down?"

"You'll be killed too," Leda said.

"We'll be gone by then," the pirate said. "This piece of shit won't rupture till after we've left your garbage vessel. Sounds to me like this reactor situation is just your problem." The pirate bent low to talk since he was so much taller than they were.

"Let us in. We can fix it," Leda said.

"I am commanded to let no one in," the man in red said.

"Damn you—we'll all die! You have to let us in!" Rosco shouted at the pirate.

The pirate stared down at Rosco. "I'll fight you for it, little man." He took a few steps back and gestured for Rosco to enter the room in front of him. The pirate paraded himself back and forth, showboating for them. His feet danced a few steps. His tight red outfit revealed a rippling set of muscles, so solid and defined that they seemed almost unnatural. "If you want it, come prove your worth to me. Let's see what you dirt farmers can do."

Rosco hesitated for a moment and took a deep breath. He had no choice. Suppressing his fear, as he'd been trained, he turned to Leda. "Get to the reactor controls once we get in there," he told her. "Eject the fuel rods as soon as possible. I'll keep him distracted."

Rosco stepped forward into the engine room and prepared to face off against the man in red. The grinning skull mask stared down at him.

He heard Leda enter the engine room behind him and saw her carefully edge her way around the chamber toward the far side.

*

Cal and the other scientists hurried down the narrow passage leading out from the back of the labs. They arrived at a small hatchway that opened to a main corridor. Cal peered out and looked around the corner. A group of three Enforcers were guarding the corridor ahead, but they seemed unaware of the passage from the labs. None were facing toward Cal. Beyond the Enforcers lay the entrance to a server room.

"That's where we need to go," Cal said.

"They'll shoot us on sight," one of the others told him. "How are we getting past them?"

Cal heard a clamor from behind them. The other Enforcer squad had breached the lab. Very soon, they would discover the small tunnel leading to the scientists' current position.

"Anyone have any ideas?" Cal asked quietly.

"I have an idea," someone said. The man crept out of cover carefully. Cal and the others fell silent and hid themselves farther back out of sight. Slowly, Cal peered out and saw the man making his way down the corridor. Another doorway was open to their right, Cal realized, with a pair of boots poking out and soaked in a pool of blood. None of the Enforcers had noticed him yet. Something rustled, and Cal shut his eyes and cringed. Then he opened them slowly. The scientist was carefully creeping back toward them, carrying a bundle of grenades and one of the Enforcers' large rifles on a shoulder strap. He returned to cover with them.

"Now what?" Cal asked.

"That's as far as I'm going with this," the scientist said. "I don't know how to use any of these things."

"I don't either," Cal said, but he took the grenades and gun. He settled the gun in his arms, its strap over his shoulder.

"Do you know how to open the door to the server room?" he asked the others.

They all nodded.

Cal looked at a grenade in his hand. "Let's, uh, knock them down with this. Then we all run inside and shut the door. We've got to be quick, no more than a second or two. If anything happens to me, remember: disconnect the servers. Unplug everything."

The other Enforcer squad was approaching from behind. Cal's heart filled with a rush of terror. He thought of Eevey and wondered if these were his last moments.

"Here we go." Cal pulled out a pin from his grenade and tossed it forward.

It scraped and bounced along the floor toward the Enforcers guarding the armory. One of them saw it and started to shout as it detonated. A bright white flash filled the corridor with searing intensity that lasted several seconds. A wind of gritty dust hit Cal in the face, and rather than hearing the sound of a blast, he felt blazing hot air burning his skin. His vision slowly returned, and where the men had been, a large hole glowed in the floor of the deck, as well as a similar hole in the ceiling above. The walls around were burned black.

"Get in there!" Cal said after a moment of shock.

The group all ran forward. The hole melted into the floor was narrow enough to jump across. Cal leapt over without looking down and landed on the far side by the door to the server room. The others jumped across and arrived next to him. One of the scientists started working on the control panel to the room.

"It's locked down," he said.

"What?" Cal asked urgently.

"There's some kind of security lock in place. I've not seen this before."

Cal swore loudly and stamped his foot in frustration. They were trapped outside a locked door, at a junction they'd just vaporized. They were even exposed above and below, thanks to the holes he'd created.

The sound of Enforcers' voices was close by. The squad from the laboratory was coming through toward them.

"Shit," Cal said. "Okay, keep working on it."

Cal jumped back over the hole and took cover behind the edge of a wall, where he had a view of the laboratory hatchway. He aimed the shotgun at the area and waited, his heart pounding. He thought of Eevey again, a flash of memory, so distant. He sweated uncontrollably, the liquid running down his fingers. An Enforcer appeared through the hatchway, and Cal pulled the trigger. The gun released an enormous boom and jumped violently in his hand. A hail of sparks erupted around the hatch entrance, as the metal was ripped up by a torrent of shrapnel. The Enforcer retreated immediately.

"How's the door coming along?" Cal shouted over his shoulder.

"We might be getting somewhere" was the reply.

"I guess I'll just stay here, then," he muttered to himself. He considered surrender but realized he'd already decided against it. "Hurry up!" he called back to the others. Cal sensed movement again at the hatchway from the labs and fired another shot at the area. He fired again. He wasn't sure if he'd hit anyone. Injuring them would be best, to slow them down. If they'd realized just one man was holding them up, they'd have already charged out and overwhelmed him. At that exact moment, two Enforcers leaned out and fired their guns at him. He flinched and scurried back from his position.

"Shit shit shit," Cal hissed. He tried to take cover behind another piece of wall farther down the corridor. Cal was back close by the other scientists, with the melted hole just behind him, and nervous at being exposed from below.

"Can some of you guys watch my back?" he asked them. "If someone is getting ready to shoot me in the ass, then…"

None of them could do anything. They had only one gun between them.

"Let me know about it, I guess…"

The Enforcers fired another burst of shots, but they hadn't realized that Cal had already retreated from his position. The wall where Cal had been sheltering was punctured by their shrapnel rounds. Cal raised his weapon and fired back at them. He heard a scream of pain from the far side of the hatchway, along with the sound of angry voices. He heard a man issuing orders, a leader preparing his squad. It was a countdown, Cal realized.

"Oh shit, we're out of time. They're all coming through right now. Open the door!" Cal yelled. He heard the mechanical squeal of the server room door opening at last. He turned around and jumped back over the melted hole once again. The other scientists had already entered. Behind Cal, a cacophony of noise erupted as the Enforcer squad burst through into the corridor behind him, all firing their weapons. The gunfire was deafening, overwhelming his senses. Cal didn't look back but dashed ahead as fast as he could. He felt a hail of sharp points tug at his clothing and cut through his skin as the barbed projectiles ripped into him. He collapsed through the doorway and tumbled into the server room, his face hitting the metal floor. The other scientists sealed the door shut behind him.

Chapter 14

Everything on the bridge was destroyed. Dead bodies and torn wiring hung out from every surface in the cylindrical space. Advocate Fargas lay on his back, his blue suit torn, covered in blood splatter, in a state of shock. The leader of the pirate band stood over him, cleaning her blade with a piece of an Enforcer's uniform.

Fargas looked around, fearful of what was about to happen. Captain Haran's body was still on the floor, unmoving.

"Is this journey going how you thought it would?" the pirate leader asked Fargas.

Despite his stress, Fargas managed to shrug slightly. "Honestly, I expected it to go a little better than this." He tried to remain calm, telling himself that he was too valuable to kill. He had no option but to hope that was true.

She laughed. "My name is Tarufa. I have a message for you."

She took off her mask so that Fargas could see her face. Her bluish skin was filled with lines and wrinkles, but gene therapy had kept her physically young. Her gray bodysuit was covered in bright orange and blue markings that looked like they'd been added in paint.

Two pirates came along and dumped Cartographer Yendos on the floor next to Fargas.

"Yendos, you greasy hermit. I know who you are," Tarufa said to Yendos's slumped form. "You should listen, too, if you know what's good for you."

Yendos groaned and attempted to roll over, but he couldn't fully manage it. Like all of them, he'd been injured in the fight. His black leather suit had shiny traces of blood from small lacerations all across it.

Tarufa squatted down in front of them both. She was so tall that she towered over Fargas as he lay supine.

"Theeran knows about the Seed of Steel," she said.

"What?" asked Fargas. That was the last thing he'd expected to hear. He was stunned.

She stood up and walked away slightly. "You heard me."

Angry voices sounded, and more pirates appeared, dragging the pilot from the entrance to the cockpit area. He looked like he'd been beaten although, Fargas noted with a clinical eye, perhaps only superficially.

"Marraz here knows all about it too. Don't you?" Tarufa asked.

Marraz didn't answer but looked at the floor and avoided eye contact.

"It brought all three of you here." She gestured at them. "I know who all of you are. The outsiders. The non–Vale Reachers. You've all followed the trail of the same thing, and you don't even realize it."

Fargas began to connect things. She couldn't have collected such information in her life as a pirate. She'd been briefed on all of them, somehow, including him. He began to devise a list of who could do that.

She walked over to Marraz. "It's been a while since we last met. Somehow, you learned what's down there on Vale Reach during your journeys in space. You are right to be afraid—it will mean the destruction of your home world. You really are here for altruistic reasons, Marraz, my young friend. You want to help these people. But you must know they're doomed."

Marraz struggled against the two pirates holding his arms, but he couldn't get free. "Tarufa, you didn't need to kill the crew here. Did you come here because of me? Is that what this is about?"

"My god, I'd forgotten how much ego you had," she said. "No, Marraz. We're not here to disrupt your new career aboard this diminutive ship," she said with amused disdain.

She turned and pointed accusingly at Cartographer Yendos. "You're no kind of altruist. Your family owe immeasurable debts. They're hostages, really. You've been searching for the ancient device as payment for a long time. You've come halfway across the galaxy to find it, mapping the forgotten transit routes to triangulate its position. Do you even know it's on Vale Reach?"

"Of course the Seed is on Vale Reach," he moaned. "I found signs of that in every system I visited. But no one can find it within that damn planet!"

"Confess to us why you are really aboard this ship," she said. "Don't make me ask unkindly." Her eyes seemed to flash for a moment. They were artificial replacements.

"Studying the actual indigenous people of Vale Reach was impossible till now. There are forensic clues in their physiology. When I discovered what these people were doing, it became obvious they would lead me to the device eventually. But what do you know of my journey? Who are you, really, and why do you know of my family?" Yendos asked Tarufa. He successfully rolled over onto his back.

"I know enough, cartographer. You want the Seed of Steel to restore your clan's power. Some seek it for personal power, Yendos. Others love to hunt the mystery. A few want the device just so that others won't have it," she said with a sinister smile. "Guessing what each player wants is all part of the fun. But me? I am a pirate and proud of it. Nothing more."

Fargas was sure the woman's loyalties went somewhere far beyond the Lizard King and his piracy, no matter what she said. She turned to Fargas, regarding him with fierce relish. "And you. The Advocate. You and I have a mutual friend," she told him.

Fargas began to understand what linked them together—Tarufa and the pilot, Yendos and himself and the crew of the ship. No coincidence had brought them there.

Fargas sat up slowly. "Why have you traveled so far to meet us?" he asked her.

"It was foolish of you to fly past the Lizard King's court. He is a capricious man. Anything could have happened. I suppose I'm here to get you out of trouble," Tarufa said. "You owe him a starship." She looked around, suddenly annoyed. "Where is Theeran?" she demanded.

"Theeran doesn't know about the device. None of them do," Fargas said. The people of Vale Reach were ignorant of the prize their planet held.

"Here I am," someone croaked. With great effort, someone heaved a pile of dead bodies from on top of themselves. Councilor Theeran slowly and unsteadily got to his feet. He clung to a railing. The man's look of defiance, despite his obvious exhaustion, was astounding.

"You know our language?" she asked him.

"A little," he said.

"Full of deception," she said in triumph. "This man has known of the Seed's existence all along. He knows its power, its potential. Don't you? I have conquered your ship. Your lives are mine now. If you value your existence, you'll lie to me no longer. What do you know of the Seed of Steel?"

"The Ambassador of the Tylder Empire hid a machine of unlimited power on Vale Reach in ancient times. Some people have heard the story. Almost none know how much is true." Theeran spoke quietly, as though struggling with pain. "I was the head of Vale Reach's secret police for many years. I've heard many forbidden messages from offworld. Do you think we're so ignorant? We know more than you think."

"You want to bury it if you find it, don't you?" she accused him.

"Yes." Theeran wheezed for a second as he leaned against a shattered computer console. "I hope it's never found. I hope it vanishes forever. I hope we're left alone, free to live and develop unharmed, without any outside forces demanding our land and people. As long as it exists, it's a curse on us."

Tarufa laughed, a shrill noise, bracing in its shrieking nature. For a half second, she wobbled almost as though she would fall over as she laughed. "You can't make something like this disappear. You don't have that power." She turned to Marraz. "How do you tolerate following this man?"

"You've been hiding aboard our ship since the Lizard King's fortress," Theeran said. "What do you want from us?"

"I want you to reach the Ruarken Senate," she said. "Well, not you, Councilor Theeran."

She threw her knife, which impaled Theeran through the chest. He fell to the floor, the blade clattering against the ground where it protruded from his back.

"No! Damn you, why?" Marraz screamed at her, still being held tightly by other pirates. "He didn't deserve that! He was trying to save Vale Reach! He just wanted a better life for us!"

"He was holding you back," she told him in a matter-of-fact tone. "He didn't understand what's going to be needed from you. We couldn't let him be running things by the time you arrive at the Ruarken Senate. He would never have agreed to the updated plan." She removed a metal clip from her hair, and it fell loose around her shoulders. "Listen to me, Marraz. You've seen the outside universe. You know the truth about this galaxy more than any of the other peasants aboard the ship. You alone among the Vale Reachers can see what needs to be done. When you get to the Ruarken Senate, offer them the Seed. Sell them the rights to own its power. They'll take your offer. You can demand good treatment for Vale Reach in exchange."

Fargas watched Marraz consider it. She was right. Fargas was impressed with her reasoning. Vale Reach already stood no chance of continuing to live as it had in the past. Becoming fully integrated with the outside universe was their only chance of long-term survival. They had to transform, to ride the wave that was coming.

Marraz looked at the floor. He was no longer fighting the other pirates but had become still. "Damn," he said.

Tarufa gave some signal to the pirates. One reached out and put a hand on Marraz's face, lifting his head so that he looked directly at Tarufa.

"This man…" She nodded dismissively toward Theeran's body. "He only understood the way things were. He wasn't capable of ending the only society that he understood. That's why he was doomed to fail. You should be thanking me for freeing you from him. You know I'm right," she told him. "Someone else will need to take leadership of this ship now. Can I rely on you to be a bad influence for me? Will you lead these people astray in their silly mission, like I've told you to?"

"Damn it." Marraz looked furious again but wasn't fighting. "Yes. You're right," he said through gritted teeth. He looked up. "It's our best hope."

"You'll have peace and security forever more," she told him in soft, sympathetic tones. "And as for you two…" She turned toward Fargas and Yendos. "Make sure they get there. Consider it your top priority."

"Is this what the Lizard King sent you to do?" Fargas asked her. He knew that wasn't true.

"Haven't you figured out yet who I really represent here, Fargas?" she asked. "No, the Lizard King is a materially minded man. I don't think he believes the Seed of Steel on Vale Reach is real though he'll get his prize today, make no mistake. But my message now does not come from him. It comes from the one who originally sent you to that little planet. We share the same master, you and I." She spent a moment gloating over him then stood up and walked away. She didn't look back as she spoke. "You have some cleaning up to do in here."

Slowly, Yendos sat up and groaned again. He turned towards Fargas. "I'm starting to question your abilities as a lawyer," he said.

*

The man in red was circling Rosco, tossing a single knife from hand to hand. His stance seemed casual, exuberant even. The skull mask gave no hint of facial expressions. Rosco saw that Leda had made it to the far side of the reactor chamber and entered a small control room through a door.

Above them, at the center of the room, Vale Reach's reactor was still pulsating blue, calm and steady. Most of its surface was clad in heavy metal plating.

"There's no need for this," Rosco said. "We don't even know each other." He knew the man would lunge for him at any moment. Rosco was facing a man that resembled an image of pure terror. Though the metal knife flashed silver, Rosco's eyes remained focused on the man's body, waiting for a move.

The pirate in red leapt forward into a spinning kick at Rosco, who raised his hands to block the blow. The man's boot crashed with explosive force against his forearms. Rosco was driven backward, but he managed to avoid staggering and stayed steady on his feet.

The pirate stepped back and began to circle him again. Though Rosco couldn't see any expression through the skull mask, the pirate seemed pleased, Rosco thought, happy his opponent hadn't been knocked down so early. Perhaps Rosco could keep the man entertained long enough for Leda to finish her task and prevent the ship's destruction. He watched the silver blade again. So far, the pirate hadn't used it. Rosco doubted that would continue. Just one blow from the knife could be fatal.

The pirate dived at Rosco, and the shining blade scythed toward his head. In the moment before it hit, he threw himself to the floor to avoid it. The pirate rolled smoothly back into a fighting stance as Rosco hurried to his feet again. The pirate suddenly sprang a fast front kick toward Rosco, who barely blocked the strike again. He just needed to buy time for whatever Leda was doing. He saw an opening in the pirate's defenses and swung a punch with all his strength that hit the pirate in the ribs. It was like punching concrete.

The silver knife swept at him again, and Rosco leapt back. The pirate kept advancing and slicing at him. Rosco desperately avoided every swing and lunge, struggling not to fall as he scrambled backward. The knife flashed as it cut through the air. Rosco grabbed a nearby metal toolbox from an engineer's station and swung it. The box struck the pirate's elbow as the man stabbed at him, sending the knife flying from the pirate's grasp. The pirate grabbed Rosco by the back of the neck and threw him across the room as though he weighed nothing. Rosco crashed headfirst into a desk. He struggled to his feet, dazed, and saw the pirate in red charging straight at him.

In desperation, Rosco grabbed some heavy tool from the desk and threw it at the skull mask. It struck the forehead and bounced off, barely slowing the pirate but seeming to break his concentration. Rosco rolled away and managed to avoid being grabbed again. The two circled each other again for a moment. The pirate seemed as thrilled as ever by the battle.

The reactor was changing color above them. The blue flashes within it developed an unmistakable purple tinge. Something was happening.

The pirate kicked Rosco again, and the impact knocked him down with the force of a cannon. He slid along the floor. The pirate pulled a second small knife from somewhere on his red body suit and threw the blade at Rosco. The knife struck him before he could react, burying deep in his thigh. Rosco screamed in pain then tried to stand up from the floor but realized it was impossible. His whole leg was out of commission. Then he heard Leda speak through his earpiece.

"Rosco, I'm going to bring down all the shields around the reactor. Get yourself into cover from it now."

"Go! Do it!" Rosco yelled.

He crawled and dragged himself under a nearby metal desk while the whirring motors of the reactor machinery moved the panels of heavy shielding away. A roaring began, an ocean of angry white noise that quickly reached deafening volume. A man was screaming distantly, a sound full of rage and regret. The noise was inhuman in length and rattling intensity. Rosco squeezed into a tight fetal position under the table. Eventually, the screech of the radioactive waves subsided. Rosco opened his eyes. He was still alive. He crawled out from his hiding place and surveyed the room around him from the floor. The pirate lay crumpled and immobile. Some kind of thick black mucus was steaming and bubbling out from the cracks in his suit, the dark liquid staining the bright-red outfit. Leda was standing in the doorway to the control room.

"I did it," she said. "I ejected the failed rod. It's safe."

Rosco lay on the floor in a pool of his own blood. "We saved the ship."

Leda hurried over to him and tried to help Rosco to his feet.

"Don't remove the knife," he said. "Just leave it for now. I can't stand on my own, but with your help, maybe I can walk."

He put both his arms around her, and together, they lifted him to his feet. Slowly, Rosco and Leda made their way to the exit from the reactor room. The door was open. Rosco felt a hand on his shoulder, hard like iron, and they were both forcefully turned around. The pirate in the red bodysuit was standing, staring at them, his face inches from theirs. He put his hand on Rosco's chest and pushed, sending Rosco flying backward through the doorway. Rosco crashed to the ground, looking back into the reactor chamber. The pirate seemed crazed, his posture manic, his hand still on Leda, as he hit the control panel and the door closed.

"No!" Rosco screamed. He dragged himself forward and beat on the door to the reactor room with his fists. "No! Damn it!" He pulled himself painfully up the wall and entered the codes to open the door, but it was no use. Rosco slid down the wall, his leg burning with agony. "No! Come out and face me! Leave her! Don't touch her!" He pounded against the door again.

*

Leda pulled away from the pirate's grip and scrambled backward. He spread his arms wide, as though welcoming her to him, his red suit dripping black ooze, then he crouched low, in a stance ready to catch her. He flexed his long fingers then charged forward at her. Leda ran from him. She sprinted away in the cylindrical room, but the tall man would be far faster than she was. Leda looked over her shoulder and saw he was only inches away behind her. She dived to the side, and he missed as he tried to grab her. Leda managed to get to her feet and scramble away, looking around, ready for the pirate again. He was unsteady on his feet, almost swaying a little. He faced off against her again, still fired up and eager, but he looked tired. He came toward her, and Leda turned to run again, but he reached out and grabbed her from behind. Both his hands were around her neck. He pushed her down, and Leda fell to the floor. His long fingers closed her windpipe like a python. Her vision of the room blurred and darkened. She couldn't see him as he was still behind her. Leda reached out blindly, and her fingers curled around the handle of something hard. She swung it behind herself with her remaining strength, and felt it strike the man. The fingers around her throat released, and Leda broke free and stumbled away from him. She turned around to see the pirate's skull mask had fallen from his face. So much black blood trailed down from his eyes and mouth that she still couldn't see any of his features. Poisoning from the radiation exposure was affecting him badly. Leda was holding a heavy wrench in her hand, and she hit him in the head with it again, swinging into his skull. He fell to the ground. She lifted the tool high and brought it down on his head a third time. Then she hit him again and again, till his head cracked open and bits of gray matter splattered her hair.

*

The door opened. Leda was standing there. Blood covered her face.

"My god, are you okay?" Rosco asked. He was still lying in a puddle of his own blood.

She nodded but didn't make eye contact.

"Is he...?" Rosco looked past her and saw the crumpled body of the red pirate. "Get out of there. Get away from him." Rosco reached out and pulled Leda through the doorway, but his grip was weak. He had to make sure everything was over.

"He's dead," Leda said. "Definitely dead."

Rosco realized they could no longer hear the sounds of battle throughout the ship. "What's happened?" he asked, looking around. "Are the Enforcers gone?"

Once again, Leda helped him up to his feet. The two of them carefully hurried along a corridor. Rosco checked around a corner. The bloodied bodies of Enforcers were everywhere, slumped against walls and littered across the floor. Leda and Rosco retrieved weapons from the bodies, still hearing no sounds of fighting. When they listened carefully, he could hear distant gunshots—very distant. They cautiously moved down another corridor toward the exterior of the ship, Rosco leaning heavily on Leda. They turned a corner and met Cal coming from another direction.

"Cal! Operator Heit, so good to see you," Rosco said. "We were successful. Are you okay?"

Cal shook his head in answer. "They've all gone, Rosco. They've gone down the tubes." He seemed confused but also relieved.

"What tubes? What are you talking about?" Rosco asked.

"The boarding tubes," Cal said.

The distant gunfire was coming from the other ship.

"Are there any pirates or Enforcers left here at all?" Rosco asked.

"I don't know," Cal said.

"We should get back to the bridge," Rosco said.

*

Cal, Leda, and Rosco were speechless as they arrived at the ruins of the bridge. None of them said anything. They didn't need to. The destruction and horror were apparent.

Dead pirates lay piled on top of Enforcers, on top of *Fidelity* crew. The only people still living were from *Fidelity*. Those able to move had dragged themselves away from the tangle of corpses in the middle of the room and were tending to each other's injuries. They sat huddled at the edge of the bridge, staring at the disaster. Cal and Leda moved Rosco to a chair near the middle of the room. Walking on the floor without stepping on human body parts was difficult.

Fargas was found sitting next to Theeran's body. He was despondent as Cal and Leda approached him. "Theeran couldn't get clear of the fighting," Fargas said sadly. "They were killing anyone in here. It was indiscriminate."

Leda moved to a console and studied the information she could find. "No pirates remaining in the corridors of the ship," she reported. "No Enforcers left alive on board either."

"Are the boarding tubes still connected?" Rosco asked. "Can we get away from them?"

"The metal claws on the boarding tubes are still gripped on tight. It might tear off the whole front of the ship," she said. "The damn harpoons are stuck in us too."

"Damn it," Rosco murmured. "We've got to separate from them." He lay back in the seat and shut his eyes, trying to manage the pain in his leg. He was starting to grow faint. "Where's the captain?"

"I've found her! Captain Haran is unconscious, but I think she's going to be okay," Cal said. He knelt next to her and checked her pulse. "She won't be able to help us for a while."

"Who's the ranking officer on the bridge?" Rosco asked.

"You are, Major," Cal told him.

He shut his eyes for a moment. "Okay." He sat up straight. "Try to break off the boarding tubes. Do it slowly. Get us disconnected from them. Marraz, can you still pilot the ship?"

Marraz gave Rosco a weary salute. He was sitting at a nearby console. "I can operate the ship from here. Do we have any maneuvering engines still operational at the front to reverse us?"

"Just about," Leda told him, checking her systems.

"Then we can make it happen," Marraz said.

The ship rumbled as it moved backward, pulling against the metal coils that linked the two vessels, both the harpoons and boarding tubes.

"No significant damage reported yet," Leda said. "The boarding tubes are... are they stretching?"

"They're unspooling," Marraz said. "On a ship like the Enforcer's vessel, the boarding tubes can reach out much further, for when they attempt a long-range interception. They'll hit their limit soon, though."

"Rotate *Fidelity* end over end," Cal said suddenly. "Let's use the nuclear thruster's heat." He looked around, excited by his idea. "We can melt through it all."

"That might work," Leda said.

"Do it," Rosco told them, weary from exhaustion.

Fidelity managed to spin around in a half circle. The boarding tubes and grappling hook cables were stretched down the length of its body, and the thruster became pointed in the direction of the Enforcer ship.

"Is it working?" Rosco asked. With the main screen of the bridge shut down, he had no data to look at.

"Not yet," Marraz reported.

"Can you get the thruster any hotter?" Rosco asked Leda.

"Aiming for maximum temperature," Leda said. "It's in poor condition after everything that's happened."

With a sudden jerk that rocked the entire ship, *Fidelity* broke free of its constraints.

"We've melted through the connections!" Leda reported.

"Incoming message! We're being hailed from the Enforcers' ship," Cal reported.

The sense of danger gave Rosco a fresh surge of energy. As the commanding officer of the ship, he had to answer the transmission. He tried to wipe the blood off his uniform. "Put it on-screen," Rosco said. "Focus our camera on me. Try and show me from the waist up," he said, gesturing to the knife in his leg. He adopted his most focused professional demeanor, despite his battered state.

The main screen activated. Many regions of the screen were damaged and scratched, with bright colors flickering wildly across its surface. Rosco could make out the face of the woman in gray, orange, and blue who'd led the pirates in their attack on the bridge.

"This is Major Rosco, of the ship *Fidelity*," Rosco said. "What are your intentions?"

She spoke words in an unintelligible foreign language.

"The Enforcer ship's laser batteries are charging!" Cal reported. "They're ready to fire on us, a concentrated blast."

"Shit," Rosco said. He turned to Fargas. "What did she say to us?"

"She is, ah, describing your hospitality as lackluster," Fargas explained.

"What?" Rosco asked in confusion.

"She said she found her stay on your ship to be a frustrating experience. Apparently, we made her mission far more stressful than it needed to be. They didn't expect us to nearly crash *Fidelity* so many times. The pirates had several serious debates as to whether they ought to seize control of us before they even launched their ambush."

"They were waiting onboard our ship, hiding the entire time?" Rosco asked.

"Since the Lizard King's court," Fargas told him.

"Why? What for?" Rosco asked.

The woman on the screen issued another series of statements in her unknown language.

"To help you pay your debts," Fargas explained. "This pirate band has seized a completely intact Enforcer cruiser, with all systems still functioning. She knew you were being followed and would soon be caught. They have the Enforcer ship's records and its communication codes. She's sending it back to the Lizard King to clear your account with him," Fargas explained.

"Are you serious?" Rosco asked. He couldn't understand why. It had to be part of a scheme. "Give her our gratitude. But why are their lasers aimed at our ship?"

The woman on the screen smiled at Rosco. From her position of superiority, she seemed to thoroughly enjoy the current moment. He heard her slowly say Marraz's name.

Marraz rotated his chair slowly to face the rest of the crew. Rosco saw the hesitation on his face as he spoke. "Those lasers are aimed at me, more than any of the rest of us. I knew this woman, years ago, when I was a pirate in this region of space. She wants me to deliver a message to you all. She's making sure I do it. It's the truth about Vale Reach. There is a weapon buried there, in ancient times, by someone known as the Ambassador of the Tylder Empire, called the Seed of Steel. The Ambassador hid it somewhere on our world for secrecy, a device of ultimate power, supposedly from her personal belongings, placed where no one would think to look for it. Our real mission is to reach the Ruarken Senate and discover how to unlock this device's power. If we allow the Ruarken to study the device, they'll help us to defeat the Universal Legion and save ourselves."

"You've always known this?" Rosco asked.

"Yes," Marraz said.

The pirate captain on the screen let out a laugh of triumph and clapped her hands together.

"They've powered down their laser weapons," Cal reported.

"That's it? They're letting us go?" Rosco asked. "Why are we being freed?"

"They want our journey to succeed," Marraz said. "There are major powers from all around the galaxy that want to take Vale Reach's buried weapon. These pirates are afraid of what it could do to disrupt the balance of power here. They don't want the Legion to get their hands on it. It's safer in our possession or with the Ruarken Senate."

"So we're finished with the Lizard King? We don't owe him any debt, then. It's over?" Rosco asked.

Fargas translated his question to the pirate captain onscreen and got an answer back.

"It's over. The Lizard King is a friend to anyone who hinders the Universal Legion. He wants his domains undisturbed. No doubt, he'll be satisfied with this impressive bounty you've sent to him. You're about to establish a professional reputation within his organization."

"We don't work for the Lizard King," Rosco said.

"That may be subjective at this point, from a legal perspective," Fargas said.

The pirate leader on the screen disappeared.

"They've just sent us a standard Enforcer greeting, with the official signature," Cal said.

On the flickering screen, they watched as the Enforcer ship withdrew, ignited its main engines, and blasted off into space.

Cal groaned and put his head down on his desk. Fresh blood was smeared across the back of his chair.

"Cal, are you hurt?" Rosco asked urgently.

"I think my backside is full of shrapnel," he mumbled. With difficulty, Cal got up from his chair and slowly lay facedown on the floor of the bridge. The back of his uniform was indeed shredded and dark with blood. "This position here actually feels so much better," he said slowly. "I'm just going to stay like this a while."

Leda stared ahead, her expression glassy and distant. She'd retreated into her own head.

Rosco looked down at the knife protruding from his own thigh. It suddenly caused him immense pain. "God damn it!" Rosco shouted. "Fuck, this hurts!"

Fargas appeared by his side. "Can I offer you some advice?"

Rosco groaned. "That's what you're here for, right?" he said through gritted teeth.

"Get us back to the Highway."

"Can we make it with our current level of damage?"

"We've regained a decent level of power from the reactor," Marraz said from his position at an engineer's desk.

Yendos had been waiting at the edge of the room. He took a seat on the bridge and waved for Rosco's attention. "Major, if we transit through the Highway, I can direct us to a hidden repair station on the far side. It'll be a safe place for us to dock for repairs."

Rosco looked at Yendos then at Marraz. "Will they take us in?"

"Those kind of stations will do the work with no questions asked," Marraz said. "We'll need some form of payment, but"—he nodded to the many bodies on the floor—"their equipment could suffice for it."

"We'll reach Ruarken in under one year if we continue on the Highway," Fargas told Rosco.

"We can even make a call back to Vale Reach at the repair center if they have encrypted FTL communication lines there," Marraz said.

"Sounds good," Rosco said. "Sounds like everything is good," he mumbled. He shut his eyes and fell unconscious.

*

When he opened them again, he didn't know how long he'd been out. "Are we okay?" Rosco gasped urgently as he woke up. "Is everything okay?" The knife had been removed from his leg, and people were bandaging him. He was disoriented.

"Everything is okay. Don't worry." Cal's voice was trying to calm him.

Rosco relaxed slightly. Cal and Leda were the ones bandaging him and treating his injuries, he realized. Leda brought him water, and he drank. He tried to express his gratitude.

"We're with you, Rosco. Don't worry," Cal said.

"Every step of the way," Leda said quietly.

Epilogue

The ship was too badly damaged to avoid time debt as they left the system. *Fidelity* wasn't capable of producing the required acceleration for an instantaneous jump when passing through the transit point, yet *Fidelity* was too damaged to remain on the Highway. The effects of relativity would propel them forward in time. Yendos and Marraz together prepared to direct them to a safe destination to hide and repair.

The risk they took was one for all of Vale Reach. Twenty-two months would pass by, they calculated. The fate of their world would be brought twenty-two months closer. But crossing the Highway brought them much of the way toward their destination. As long as the home world held out, the mission could succeed. They had no alternative. They would carry on to the Ruarken High Senate.

*

Fidelity had arrived at the repair station, high above an ocean world. The ship was being rebuilt at a dock facility inside a truly massive orbital shipyard.

Rosco and Marraz stood on a balcony in one of the station's workshop zones. They watched a handful of welding teams working their way along the side of *Fidelity*, removing damaged hardware and sealing breaches in *Fidelity*'s surface. As they'd hoped, they'd managed to afford basic repairs by selling much of the equipment left by the deceased pirates and Enforcers. They'd even had enough for new maneuvering engines to replace the ones lost, as well as refurbishment of their reactor.

Rosco was angry. He wasn't sure of the target of his anger, but after learning how many crew had been killed, he wasn't capable of any other response. Perhaps he was angriest at himself. "It could have been far worse," Rosco repeated. He kept telling himself it was true, like a mantra.

"No doubt," Marraz agreed.

"One quarter of the crew are gone," Rosco said bitterly. "Hard to believe that's a situation we escaped lightly from. It seems no one stationed in the engine room has survived. That means Leda is probably our chief engineer now."

"These are very dangerous people we were dealing with," Marraz said. "We could easily all have been killed. I'm telling you—as many of us as possible made it out of there alive."

"That's a fucking sad statement," Rosco said.

"You couldn't have done a better job of protecting us, Major," Marraz said. "You did everything right. You were a great soldier."

They were quiet for a moment, but the tension he felt wouldn't allow him to accept what Marraz had said. "We can't allow anything like this to ever happen again. We need to develop better ways to protect ourselves."

"Conditions should be better on this side of the Highway," Marraz said. "The Enforcers don't have jurisdiction to come through after us."

"We need weapons," Rosco said.

"An energy shield too," Marraz agreed.

They watched the unhurried work of the dockyard repairmen.

"If only wishing for them made it so." Rosco sighed in dissatisfaction. "Captain Haran is recovering well," he said after a moment. "Soon, she can supervise the refit procedure."

"And you'll be relieved of command as our acting captain," Marraz said with a sly smile.

"That's fine with me," he said. "Councilor Theeran's diplomatic aides are working with Fargas to prepare our case for the Ruarken Senate. Now that we know of the device, some adjustments are being made to the plan. Now I'm the most senior security officer aboard. It's an enormous responsibility. We really have no idea what might be out there, ready to maul this ship or crew..." He hesitated. "It's not that I'm afraid, but…"

"Use the fear, Rosco," Marraz said. "Let it make you faster and stronger."

Rosco considered Marraz's point. "I wasn't exactly trained that way. In the military, we suppress fear."

"I remember when I first reached space, how impossible and terrifying it all felt." Marraz looked out across the hangar as he spoke. "I was born on Vale Reach, you know. I lived there with my mother until I was ten years old. My father was a void-kin traveler. He used to visit Vale Reach in secret, every few years, to see me. One day, he told me it was time to go with him and see the 'real worlds,' as he called them. He was right—there is a greater existence out there, a super-reality beyond what we experience if we stay home. But Vale Reach is real too. It's where our families are. There's nothing more real in this universe than the people we love."

"I hope we're serving them well," Rosco said. "I'm concerned about the repercussions of us killing the Enforcers."

"You didn't kill the Enforcers. Tarufa's crew did that," Marraz said.

"I doubt the Enforcers will see it that way," Rosco said. "God alone knows what that Tarufa woman told the Lizard King about us. Are we a charity case to her?"

"The Enforcers' deaths could cause us problems," Marraz acknowledged. "We'll make *Fidelity* as unrecognizable as we can here. There are ways to change most of what makes us identifiable."

"Will the Enforcers come here searching for us?" Rosco asked.

Pricks of light flared across *Fidelity* in the hangar bay as welders did their jobs.

"They might venture here, but this station is sworn to a code of secrecy with clients. It's about a matter of honor for these people—absolute, assuming you're a paying customer. They'll never give the Enforcers any information. This place even has the means to defend itself. We should be hidden here till we launch again."

Rosco turned and studied Marraz, though the other man didn't face him. "There's been something I've been meaning to ask you," Rosco told him.

"Oh yeah? What?"

"Why did Councilor Theeran go to such lengths to keep you separated from the rest of the crew? They wanted you far away from all the civilians."

Marraz looked at him and smiled as though remembering a distant memory. "Because I'm a bad influence."

*

Leda arrived at a metal door with a dirty neon sign above. She knocked, and it slid open for her to enter. She passed through and entered a small machine workshop. Leda couldn't afford anyone on the main strip of workshops. She'd had to find someone down-market to accept her offer of bartering in exchange for their services. Leda sat down at a square table. An old man was sitting on the far side, waiting to receive her. Leda took out a small canvas bag and placed a series of metal objects on the table.

"You know you can never come back from this?" the old man said. "Some of these implants here… they can never fully be removed."

"I know," Leda said.

The old man was a local mechanic on the station, and he'd agreed to her price. "You are pristine," he said. "That's rare to see. You've managed to get this far through life without getting involved in cybernetics. Are you certain you want to break that clean streak?"

Leda remembered how she'd felt with the red pirate's hands squeezing around her neck. Never again. Leda had extracted the implants from his corpse herself and studied them carefully. They were sophisticated augmentations, similar items to those she'd seen onboard the space station over Paxis Prime. Some would go into her spine, enhancing her reaction times, some into her arms, some into her head. She would become faster, more precise with every decision and action, impossible to corner, enlightened, and afraid of no one. She would never be returning to her life in Vale Reach.

"Do it. I'm ready."

*

Official reports had already been sent back to Vale Reach using the FTL communication lines of the repair station. The home world's government was successfully briefed on everything that'd happened. The situation back home seemed to have remained precariously stable. The crew had a chance to make brief personal calls whilst the ship underwent its extensive repairs.

Cal called Eevey immediately. For a moment, he hesitated before he hit the button to connect. He had no idea what kind of reaction he would get. It'd been two years for her and, for him, only three months. Cal didn't know if he was delusional to hope everything would be fine. Irreversible things had happened. Eevey answered the call and appeared as an image on the screen, sitting at the kitchen table in the flat they'd shared together. She smiled at the sight of him, but she seemed sad about something too.

"Eevey! It's so good to see you! I'm so sorry about how long has passed. Are you okay?" he asked.

"I'm okay, Cal. It's good to see you too." She looked pleased, but for a moment she struggled to speak. "I'm just happy that you all made it. I never believed that the ship had been destroyed, even when we heard nothing at all from you."

"Yeah." Cal shook his head in disbelief. "We've been through a lot. I guess we've survived some tough encounters. We've got to keep on going." He laughed nervously. His heart was pounding, but he felt such relief to see her. He didn't know what to say, but just talking felt so important. "It's been two years for you."

"More than that," Eevey said, and all her sadness returned. She seemed pensive, as though she was holding something back. "This journey's going to take longer than we thought."

"Are you...? It's hard to imagine how the time's passed. It's not even been four months for me. Are we okay?" he asked her hesitantly.

"Yes, we are," she said. "I'm still with you, Cal."

Cal released a breath of relief. "Thank you. I know part of me is selfish, calling you like this. You must've thought I was dead. No call for two years. Maybe you've moved on with your life. And then, suddenly, here I am, calling you out of the blue, back from the dead, expecting you to deal with my problems. I'm selfish—I'm sorry," he began to speak faster as he talked. "I don't know if it was right for me to call you like this, but I needed to hear your voice so much. I miss life with you, Eevey. I miss everything. I miss the sun and the sunlight. I miss our old room together." He closed his eyes and shook his head. "Such terrible things have happened. I can't tell you what I've done. It's awful. I'm so sorry. Oh, god, I never meant to harm anyone. You deserve better than me. I wish I could take it all back. I'd take back everything. I wish I could just be back with you. I wish I'd stayed in that flat, and none of this had happened." Tears were streaming down his face.

"There's no need to live in fear, Caladon Heit." Another voice appeared on the call. It was soft, almost like music but somehow unnatural.

"Who's that?" he asked in concern.

An older woman came into view on the screen, standing behind Eevey in the kitchen. She wore an ornate purple dress, and she seemed somehow much larger than normal, as though double a human's size. Her face was smooth, but something seemed strangely precise about the way she looked at him. "I will provide guardianship over all of your world," the woman said.

She reached out and put a long arm around Eevey's shoulders, as though consoling her. Eevey didn't pull away but maintained a polite distance from the woman. Eevey was afraid of her, Cal realized. He wondered how this person could have arrived on Vale Reach and entered their lives.

The strange woman continued to speak. "As I once did back in my youth, I've allowed myself the time to experience the remarkable beauty of your world again, with its green mountains and crystal-clear skies. It's a surprise for me to believe I had forgotten such a trivial but satisfying detail, and I am rarely surprised. How fortunate that I was able to hide my treasure in this paradise."

"You are…" Cal stopped, uncertain if he should say it.

"I am the Ambassador of the Tylder Empire," she said.

"Why are you in my flat? What are you doing with Eevey?" Cal asked in confusion. He felt as though the ground was spinning beneath him.

"I'm here getting to know the locals, understanding this place, so I can ensure the preservation of your culture and keep this land run by your own people. So there's no need for your mission, you see?"

"You had to come into my flat specifically for that?" Cal asked. "Are you okay, Eevey? Is everything all right?"

"I'm fine," Eevey said quickly.

The Ambassador smiled. It seemed mechanical but somehow also very sincere. "Eevey and I work together now. I made her an offer, and she agreed. I'm putting her expertise to use. She has a gifted intellect and a promising career. But you are correct—that does not explain why I'm in your flat. I'm here, Cal, specifically because I needed to make contact with someone on your mission. I've studied profiles of all of the crew of your ship. You are the one most likely to see reason, Cal. Eevey agrees. You need to tell the others that your journey doesn't have to continue. I can solve your problems."

Cal hesitated. He couldn't say anything that would jeopardize the mission. "What do you know about the ship?"

"I know everything. I must warn you that if you continue to persist in this journey, I will be forced to direct my agents to terminate it for you. Don't go any farther. Please. I'm asking you in the name of kindness. Are you so determined to throw your life away? I don't want to slaughter you all," the Ambassador said. "I hope you truly appreciate how I've chosen to use my time to tell you that myself, in person."

"Could you protect us from the Universal Legion?" Cal asked, wondering if she was exactly what they'd been searching for.

"The Legion are not the worst of your problems," she said.

"What does that mean?" he asked.

"I am here in the house of this fine young woman, on this video call, to remind you that the Makron Empire is coming. Billions of them. You cannot imagine the scale of Makron civilization. Even I've only ever seen the surface of their mass. They are on their way. That is one of the few things beyond my power to control. Remember that. And they do not stop to appreciate beauty, as I do. They will reach this world. Are you so sure you can afford to reject the embrace of the Universal Legion?"

Cal remembered the images he'd seen of the worlds owned by the Universal Legion, burned and polluted to a wasteland. He thought of what little he knew about the Ruarken Senate and the ancient device on Vale Reach.

"You'd allow the Legion to take over control of our world?" he asked her.

"Cal, the Legion taking over management of your planet is inevitable," she said.

Cal shook his head. "We didn't get this far just to give up."

He thought of Vale Reach's options. If they could reach the Ruarken Senate, they could trade the rights to the device for their protection and demand safe conditions for Vale Reach. They could avoid colonization by the Universal Legion. He'd seen maps that showed the Makron Empire was decades away, if not longer. They would have time to find some way to deal with the Makron. They still had hope for preserving their world, perhaps more hope than ever before.

"If we were going to accept colonization by the Legion, we would never have left home," Cal told the Ambassador.

"Is this a wise choice you're making?" she asked.

Cal looked at Eevey, who still had the Ambassador's hands on her shoulders. Eevey and the Ambassador had planned this conversation in advance, he realized, working together. And yet as Cal looked into her eyes, he saw she still truly wanted to help him. That was all genuine.

"Think about it, Cal. Think of the alternatives you have," said the Ambassador. "I'm giving you this chance to surrender and prevent any more carnage for your ship. Remember, I want the best outcome for you."

"Didn't you just… weren't you threatening to kill me only a moment ago?" Cal asked, stammering slightly.

"Only professionally speaking," the Ambassador replied.

Cal blinked incredulously. He had no idea how to respond to that.

"We don't know each other personally, yet, Caladon. But we will." The Ambassador disconnected the call.

*

Fargas looked at the assembled crew with a sense of genuine admiration. They'd gathered together in an open space on the repair station to pay their final respects to Councilor Theeran and the other dead with a memorial ceremony. *Fidelity* had no space for corpses, and the bodies had already been released into space not long after their deaths. Instead, a folded flag from Vale Reach was placed at the center of the memorial. It was a fitting symbol for Theeran. His life had been filled with service and duty until the moment it was over.

The crew had become hardened. Every one of them had faced death and escaped where others hadn't. That knowledge would change them permanently, whether they fully realized it or not. They'd seen blood flowing in the most literal sense. It divided them from those who had not.

Fargas kept his head bowed out of respect, but he surveyed the bridge crew. Major Rosco had led the ship through its darkest hour. Bandages were still wrapped around his wounds, but he stood with military stiffness. Leda Palchek had become the chief engineer. More than the others, she had begun to leave behind the ways of Vale Reach. That was good. Even Operator Caladon Heit had overcome his fears and proven what he was capable of. He would again prove capable when needed, Fargas suspected.

The ceremony was ending. The crew were silently departing to go about their own business. They'd become so much more than what they were just months ago. They would need to continue to grow, and quickly, if they wanted to use the Ruarken Senate to preserve their world. Yet perhaps things were coming together as he'd hoped. Since the ship had crossed the Highway, the people of Vale Reach would be unknown on this side. The Ruarken Senate was in reach for them. As Tarufa had correctly said, success would require the right people at the helm when they arrived. And they would need to arrive soon. Fargas's master had been very clear. The Ambassador was to be prevented from recovering her device by any means necessary.

The Infinite Void series

Infinite Void is a science fiction space-opera series, focused on a far future galaxy of dysfunctional cyberpunk empires and frontier societies.

Danger and suspense fill each exhilarating encounter. Many brave souls will fail. Only a tenacious few will reach their goals and achieve unimaginable power.

All will bear witness to the wonders and terrors brought by mankind's inevitable transformation.

The next stage of human evolution faces chaos.

Defiant Space – Novel One

One starship against the galaxy.

When an armada of predatory warships come to annex their world, the inhabitants of planet Vale Reach must face the fearsome threats that stalk their galaxy. Terrors lurk in the uncharted depths of space, ready to crush their world and enslave its people. A lone starship is sent on an impossible journey. But is it already too late?

Caladon Heit wants to prevent the destruction of everything he knows. Together, the ship's crew must overcome the ferocious marauders and brutal empires that seek to eradicate them all.

In space, they will find a harsh and remorseless environment. Unimaginable enemies await behind every moon and asteroid. Their mission will demand sacrifices from every crew member to reach its destination. Will they emerge with their resolve and their starship intact? Or will

Fidelity and their homeworld be annihilated?

Defiant Space is the first novel in the Infinite Void series.

Defiant Systems – Novel Two

One starship against endless empires.

The starship Fidelity arrives on the far side of the galaxy, without power or allies. A fiery interstellar conflict threatens to pull them in. Fidelity must find a way through the complex web of loyalties needed to survive on the frontlines of a warzone.

Cal is haunted by dreams of a ruthless ancient being that hunts them. His comrades, Rosco and Leda, must master the advanced technology around them, and begin a perilous journey down the path of cybernetic augmentation.

Only through their ingenuity and wit can the travellers from Vale Reach hope to defy the odds and achieve their impossible mission. War machines and horrors of titanic scale will rise against them in an epic confrontation as they draw nearer to the prize of securing protection for their homeworld.

Can the crew of Fidelity face the full onslaught of a hostile galaxy? Or will they become just another casualty in an endless struggle between empires?

Defiant Systems is the second novel in the Infinite Void series.

Inhuman Pressure - Anthology One

An anthology of nine short stories of interplanetary conspiracy and catastrophe.

Cybernetic elder beings control the stars. Haunted wilderness planets offer no safety. The limits of the human condition are tested as ordinary people face conquest and revenge.

An impending apocalypse. A lone soldier at the end of a galaxy. Witness the fate of the universe in a startling collection of science fiction tales. A trail of forgotten lives will have vast consequences for all civilization.

Inhuman Pressure is the first anthology in the Infinite Void series.

Recurrent Immortality - Anthology Two

An anthology of nine short stories of cosmic discovery and survival in space.

The void between planets is filled with pirates and hunters seeking their fortune in the lawless chaos of the galaxy's frontiers. Unhinged ship captains, haunted machines and inhuman hybrids stalk the path of unwary travelers to the stars.

A handful of desperate souls will experience incredible transformations to escape death and become greater than human.

Recurrent Immortality is the second anthology in the Infinite Void series.

Join our newsletter for exclusive access to 'The Survivors' – a prologue short story to the Infinite Void series.

Plus early reading access, discounts on new releases, and more exclusive bonus content:

Join here:

https://cutt.ly/rimington

About the Author: Richard Rimington

Richard Rimington is a British author living in Hong Kong. He is a writer of science fiction, working for over fifteen years.

His favorite authors include Phillip K. Dick, Alastair Reynolds, Dan Simmons and Ann Leckie.

Get regular updates at
https://rimmblog.wordpress.com/

RICHARD RIMINGTON

Acknowledgements

Thank you, Indrani Banerjee, Paul Rodgers, Matt Harris and Dan Schaefer for reading and reviewing early drafts

Thank you, Michele Koh Morollo, Paul Corrigan, and Jervina Lao for providing critique

Thank you to editors Lynn, Sara and Kelly Reed at Red Adept Editing.

Thank you to cover artists Kim and Jovana at https://www.derangeddoctordesign.com/

Thank you Matt Guntrip, Kate Abbott and Fred Oskarsson for advising with cover design.

Printed in Great Britain
by Amazon